FAMOUS LAST WORDS

A DCI HARRY MCNEIL NOVEL

JOHN CARSON

DCI SEAN BRACKEN SERIES

CALVIN STEWART SERIES

DI FRANK MILLER SERIES

Crash Point
Silent Marker
Rain Town
Watch Me Bleed
Broken Wheels
Sudden Death
Under the Knife
Trial and Error
Warning Sign
Cut Throat
Blood from a Stone
Time of Death

Frank Miller Crime Series – Books 1-3 – Box set
Frank Miller Crime Series - Books 4-6 - Box set

SCOTT MARSHALL SERIES

Old Habits

FAMOUS LAST WORDS

This one is for all the hard working men and women - and animals - of Police Scotland

ONE

'It's beautiful, isn't it?' Alex said, stepping up to her husband.

Detective Chief Inspector Harry McNeil was looking at the sun glancing off the surface of the loch. He turned to look at her again, just like he'd done so many times in the past couple of hours, and every time he did, he thought that she was a figment of his imagination and if he blinked, she wouldn't be there. That she would still be dead.

But she was right there, back at his side, larger than life.

'It is,' he said, about to drop a corny line like 'but not as beautiful as you', but it was too soon.

Since Neil McGovern had dropped the bombshell this morning, Harry had felt cold and numb.

McGovern had said last night there was going to be a surprise and to be up bright and early. And this was the surprise. The best surprise Harry had ever had.

Alex stepped forward and put her hand through his arm.

'Is the red hair permanent?' he asked her.

'Do you want it to be permanent?' She smiled at him, teasing.

'No, I think I prefer you to be blonde.' He looked back out across the water, a million questions racing through his mind, but he didn't want to overwhelm her.

'You hungry?' she asked.

'Not really. I feel like a wee boy who's been waiting for months to go on holiday to Blackpool, and now he's at the bus about to get on and he doesn't know what seat to take.'

She laughed, and it was like it had only been yesterday since he had last heard it.

Then the punch in the guts again. The question he kept asking himself, over and over again: *Does she know about Morgan?*

Not for the first time, he felt like turning and walking away. There would be no awkward questions to answer that way. On the one hand, he was more than elated to see his wife again, but on the other hand, he had been in a relationship up until yesterday. When Morgan died.

No, he couldn't think of Morgan as dying; she had been shot dead by a marksman in his house as she had tried to kill him. That was something that he couldn't just drop into the conversation.

McGovern had said that there would be a team of people who were going to sit down with them, together and apart, and help them adjust. Harry had just been fed breadcrumbs, and he wondered whether Alex had been told that her husband had moved on.

Harry heard the scuff of a shoe on the rocks leading down to the shore and turned to see McGovern approaching. He wasn't a tall man, but what he lacked in height he more than made up for in stature.

'I don't know about you two, but I'm famished,' he said. 'I have one of my crew making soup and sandwiches. And a cup of tea, of course.'

It was McGovern's subtle way of asking them to join him in the cottage.

'Now that you mention it, some soup might be just the thing,' Harry said, and moved away from Alex.

She seemed taken aback for a second, but

McGovern made eye contact with her and slightly shook his head.

This was a great weight on Harry's shoulders, and right now he was doing a good job of mentally processing having his wife back in his life. He walked up the rough track that led to the back of the cottage. He wanted to start asking Alex questions, but he knew they would come out thick and fast, so he held back. Alex had asked him how her baby was and he had told her Grace was doing well. And he'd left it at that for now.

Inside, the air was cooler. A member of McGovern's staff had put out three bowls of tomato soup and laid out some chicken sandwiches before leaving them alone. The mugs of tea were already on the table.

'Let's have our lunch and we'll talk more,' McGovern said.

When it was done, they sat back and Harry focused on McGovern. He wanted to look at Alex, but felt he couldn't take his eyes off her and didn't want to seem to be staring.

'When I told you that Alex was still alive, you remember what you said to me?' McGovern said.

Harry nodded. 'I asked you what the hell you were talking about.'

McGovern smiled and nodded. 'You did. And I told you that she was still alive and living it up in the Highlands. That she was being protected by my people. I also said that I would explain in more detail when we got here. I didn't want to overwhelm you, Harry. I know it's a shock. You saw your wife's coffin being lowered into the ground. But it had to look that way. Everything we did had to look authentic, to make it look like Alex was dead.'

'Mission accomplished.' Harry looked over at Alex and realised there had been anger in his voice, which had not been intended.

'Think of today as the first day on a long road, Harry,' McGovern said.

Alex reached over and put a hand on Harry's. He saw her eyes were gleaming and smiled at her, squeezing her hand.

'It's going to be a huge adjustment for us both,' she said to her husband.

'I know.'

She didn't let go as McGovern spoke again.

'Harry, one thing on your mind, I know, is *why?* You've already asked me several times, and I said I would explain to you, and it's an explanation that you deserve.' McGovern sipped his tea. 'You want to know why I faked your wife's death and let you live a lie for the best part of a year. There's a simple answer: to protect Grace and yourself.'

Harry gently slipped his hand away from his wife's. A question ran through his mind: *What if I'd wanted to marry Morgan after a couple of months? Would you have intervened?* Yet he knew now that was exactly what would have happened.

'Her life was in danger?' he asked quietly.

'It was to do with Alex and Jessica's father,' McGovern said. 'As you know, he was a killer. After he killed his wife and took his own life, his personal belongings were gone through and it was discovered that there was a credible threat to Alex's life. It went up the chain of command and Percy Purcell got to hear of it, and since he knew me through Frank Miller, he gave me a call.'

Percy Purcell had been a detective superintendent and a good friend of Miller's, but he had gone on to higher things at Tulliallan.

'It was the hardest thing I've ever had to do, leaving you and Grace behind,' she said to Harry.

'We thought that this might have been a hoax, or the ramblings of a madman,' McGovern said, 'but we also knew he had some dodgy associates. I didn't want to take the risk.'

'Turns out the bastard wanted me dead too,'

Harry said. He looked at McGovern. 'Could you give us a minute?'

'Of course. Take your time.'

The older man got up from the table and left the room. It was warm, the sunlight streaming through the kitchen window, and Harry took a breath for a moment.

'This is hard,' he said to Alex.

'Hard for both of us.'

He held up a hand, wanting to get this out before he found his throat clamping shut. 'How much did Neil tell you about what went on back home?'

'He told me that two people were killed. One of them a woman.'

'Did he tell you about her?'

Alex nodded. 'Morgan Allan was your lover.' She spoke in a quiet voice.

Harry could feel his cheeks going red. 'I didn't intend to get into another relationship –'

She reached over and put a hand on his. 'I knew the pitfalls before I got into this. Faking my death meant you were a widower in everybody's eyes, so why wouldn't you find somebody else? I knew it was a risk. If you suddenly announced you were getting married, then Neil would have stepped in. Your name was flagged in the system to alert him of that possibility. I would be lying if I said it doesn't hurt, but I have to move forward from this point, not dwell on what happened. I did what I did to keep my baby safe. And you. I had to put myself into a different mindset. You had a relationship, but you thought I was dead. It wasn't something you did when we were married. I don't blame you, Harry, and from this day on, we have a second chance. But only if you want me.'

'Of course I want you. It's going to take a bit of adjusting, and time to accept the fact that you're not dead. But we can do it together.'

Alex smiled at her husband. 'Now that I've come back from the grave, how about taking me home to see my little girl?'

TWO

Brenda O'Brian would have been the first to admit that she needed to drop a few pounds, and her doctor had told her to take up some form of exercise, and not just lifting the TV remote. Tom had told her this walk was 'just a wee wander through the woods', but now she realised he was a lying bastard.

Brenda and Tom were in their early forties and had been dating for just over a year. Tom lived at home with what Brenda liked to call 'the old witch' but Tom lovingly referred to as his mother. The first time Brenda had been introduced to the old woman, she had overheard her talking with Tom in the kitchen in barely disguised whispers, and the witch had told Tom that she thought Brenda was built like the side of a house. Brenda knew that she should have hit the gym instead of hitting the couch and hearing that remark had spurred her on. She had even walked to the gym, promising herself that one day she would go in and sign up.

When Tom had suggested they go and visit Prince Albert's Cairn, she had been about to blurt out, 'What cairn?' but didn't want to show her ignorance. Instead, she had said that would be smashing, hoping that there would be some sort of café up at the summit, but Uncle Google had told her that there was no such thing, and it was a forty-minute walk uphill through the woods.

Forty minutes! Christ, she could scoff down two Greggs sausage rolls and a bottle of Irn-Bru in less than that! And more to the point, was there a lift? Even some kind of ski lift would be fine. The thought of sitting in one of those rickety death traps to strap two pieces of wood to your feet and narrowly avoid death at the hands of a tree while shooting downhill with no brakes just didn't have any appeal. But getting up there without breaking sweat, now she could handle that, with a lazy stroll back down after snapping a few photos of the pile of stones.

'A pile of fucking stones!' she had wanted to

shout. If she wanted to look at a pile of stones, she could go and look at the wee mound of gravel that had been sitting in her dad's back garden for two years as he contemplated laying some slabs. That man – God bless his heart! – had taught her the mantra, *Why do today what you can put off until tomorrow?*

Now they were God knows how far up this fucking trail and she had lost sight of Tom and her knickers were sticking to her with sweat. She was sure that some wee bastard bugs were nibbling on every bit of exposed skin she had, and she was trying to decide whether she should tell Tom that they were finished, or just go for Plan B and call the police and tell them he had fallen and banged his head on a rock and God rest his soul. Maybe kick him in the bollocks first.

Her leg muscles felt the same way they had when she'd stupidly believed Tom that it would be fun to climb to the top of the Scott Monument. All those skinny stone steps, turning round in the confined space. She had got to the top and looked out, wondering if anybody would know where the projectile vomit had come from. Tom had thought her fright was a real hoot.

By the time she had managed to get down without breaking her neck, she had felt like breaking his. He had laughed at her when she said her legs felt like she had bench-pressed a small car, and in that moment in time she'd wondered if Tom had a good dentist.

He had taken her out to dinner at a restaurant of her choice after that, and she had damn well made sure that it was an expensive one. She had watched him smile at the bill and waited for him to laugh at that, but of course he didn't. She dabbed at the corners of her mouth and told him that she was absolutely exhausted after that day's adventure.

After that, Tom hadn't asked her to do anything more strenuous than walk up the length of a coach.

Until today.

His idea of a stroll through the woods was a lot different from hers. She could feel the burn again, just like the time she had used an exercise bike for the first time, the lactic acid making her feel like she was on fire.

She would give him fire when she caught up.

She looked at the ground all the way up, trying not to trip over a jutting wee stone and break an ankle. Scenarios were going through her head, every one of them involving her standing at Tom's funeral, accepting people's condolences. She didn't know who she hated more, Tom for putting her through this or herself for allowing him to put her through this.

As she came out of the woods looking like she had been wandering through the mountains for weeks, she spotted him standing at the corner of the cairn.

'There you are,' she said. 'Thanks for waiting.'

He didn't say anything in return, or even turn round to acknowledge she was there. Brenda thought how easy it would be to belt the back of his head with a rock right now.

'Hey, Tom! Hello! I'm actually here? Or are you on your phone again? Wee bastard.'

She walked closer to him, but still he said nothing. Then she stepped beside him and saw what he was looking at: a young female sitting slumped backwards against the huge stone cairn.

'Jesus,' she said. Tom was pale and shaking.

Brenda took her phone out and was relieved to see there was a bar on the screen. She called the police and assured the despatcher that the girl was clearly dead, there was lots of blood and no, she wouldn't fucking well try to see if there was a pulse.

She ended the call and walked past Tom to wait

at the edge of the woods, where the corpse was out of sight.

'Oh, and by the way,' she said as she passed Tom, 'we're finished. Wanker.'

THREE

When Harry opened his front door, he didn't know what to expect. Would the smell of blood still be lingering? Or the smell of gunpowder? Would there be remnants of the carnage that had been here before he left?

He, Jessica and Grace had spent the previous night in a safe house in Juniper Green. Harry had left for the airport straight from there, his life in somebody else's hands. A private jet to Inverness, then driven in a big SUV to the cottage by the loch.

He turned to look at Alex, and McGovern right behind her. He wasn't a hundred per cent convinced that it was over. Probably wouldn't be for the rest of his life.

'The crew were in all night cleaning up,'

McGovern assured him. 'You would never know unless you were there.'

Harry nodded and walked in, then stood by the door while Alex joined him.

'I'm scared, Harry,' she whispered.

'It'll be fine,' he said. He looked over at McGovern again. They'd talked on the jet down, about how Jessica was being briefed by McGovern's daughter – and DI Frank Miller's wife – Kim Miller.

And then Jessica stepped into the hall from the living room, her eyes red. She couldn't speak, but merely held out her arms, and Alex rushed into them and they both started crying. McGovern came in and closed the door.

After a few moments, Jessica still couldn't speak, but they parted and Alex stood on the threshold of the living room before entering.

And there she was, the little girl she'd left behind a long time ago. Kim Miller was holding her in her arms.

'Welcome home, Alex.' She smiled and held out Grace for her mum, and the little girl smiled as Alex took hold of her.

They were at the start of a long road, like marathon runners waiting for the word to go. Grace would go on as she had since the very day that Alex had left the mortuary in the Western General hospital, coordinated by McGovern and his people. Alex would slowly integrate herself back into her daughter's life, with help from Harry and Jessica.

'I don't know about you lot, but I feel like a cup of tea. Anybody else?' McGovern said.

They all agreed that they did.

'Harry, I'd like to ask you to show me to your kitchen, son, but since I know where it is already, feel free to join me.'

When the two men were in the kitchen waiting for the kettle to boil, McGovern stood leaning against the counter and said, 'How does it feel now that Alex is back home?'

'Weird. I mean, Alex supposedly died in the flat in Comely Bank. She didn't live here. I had to grieve for her, I ran away to deal with it, left my baby with Jessica, came back, started a relationship with a woman who wasn't what she seemed, and now I find out that my wife wasn't dead at all but in protective custody. It's a lot to deal with, Neil.'

McGovern clapped a hand on Harry's shoulder. 'I know it is, son. If I didn't think you could handle it, I wouldn't have broken it to you this way, but you're a strong man.'

'Try telling that to Jessica. When I bought a

house down in the south of Scotland, I didn't intend to come back.'

'But you did. And now you can get on with your life with Alex. If that's what you want. I told you that yesterday too. This has to be your choice as well. Alex understands that. She and I had a good talk, on more than one occasion, even before we put this plan into action, and she was willing to go ahead with it if it meant keeping Grace safe.'

'It very nearly had a different outcome.' Harry looked at the older man. 'Your men are expert shots.'

'They've had a lot of experience. They don't miss.' The kettle reached the boil and McGovern made the tea. 'I know you've hardly had time to process the situation with Morgan,' he said, his back still to Harry as he poured. 'How do you feel?'

'My head's spinning. One minute I have a girl-friend, and the next I find out that she was in love with somebody else and just using me. Now she's dead, and a woman who was my wife, who I thought was dead, is in the same room where Morgan sat just minutes before she died. To say that my mind is fucked is putting it mildly.'

McGovern laughed. 'Can you get the milk?'

Harry fetched the carton from the fridge and put it next to McGovern on the counter.

'I don't know how Alex takes her tea anymore,' Harry said.

'Milk and no sugar. Does that sound about right?'

'It does.'

Harry wondered if anything else had changed with his wife. Then a thought occurred to him. 'I need to know something and I don't feel comfortable asking Alex.'

McGovern turned to look at him. 'You want to know if she had a relationship with another man.' He shook his head. 'No, she didn't. Simon Gregg and Steffi Walker were with her every time they went out socially. Alex knew that was part of the deal. Those two colleagues were her bodyguards. Even though they're police officers, they've been through extensive additional training in protection. Easier for Steffi, I must say, as she's ex-army. But Simon has the height advantage. So, unless Alex sneaked out at night, the answer is no. She always clung on to the fact that one day she would be going home. And she loves you and Grace more than anything. She didn't want anybody else, Harry, just you.'

Harry felt relief and guilt at the same time. 'I told Alex about Morgan and we talked it through, but I have no doubt that sometime in the future, maybe when I've pissed her off, she'll bring it back up.'

McGovern poured the milk and handed the carton back to Harry. 'That couldn't have been easy, but a psychologist had mentally prepared Alex for that possibility.'

They took the five mugs through to the living room, where Alex was bouncing Grace up and down on her knee.

They sat around chatting.

'I can't thank you enough for looking after Grace,' Alex said to her sister. And then, as if on cue, Grace reached her arms out for Jessica, who came across and took her.

'It's going to be a transition,' Kim said, watching tears spring into Alex's eyes.

'I know.'

'It's going to be hard, and that's something we spoke about many times, but take a look at your daughter, Alex: she's alive. That's because you made the selfless decision to go away for a while.'

Jessica smiled at Alex. 'It's going to be okay. We'll do this together, sis.'

'Thank you. I appreciate you all doing this for me. For us.' Alex looked at Harry and smiled. Then she stood up. 'Harry, can I talk to you for a minute?'

Harry nodded and they left the living room and went through to the kitchen.

'Listen, I know this is a shock for you, so I can have Neil let me stay in a safe house here in Edinburgh, if that makes you feel more comfortable.'

Harry looked at her for a moment. 'This is our home. If you want to stay here, I don't have a problem with it. But I have to say, just for now, I would feel more comfortable if we had separate bedrooms.'

'I understand. I'll stay here and then further down the road...' She left the sentence unfinished.

'That's something I have to work on.'

'One day at a time,' she said and gave him a hug, and he held on tightly.

'One day at a time,' he agreed.

After what felt like a lifetime, they parted, Harry feeling that he was going to wake up from a dream, but no, this was real.

Neil McGovern came into the room. 'I've just had a phone call. I need to go, but we'll talk later. About going back on duty, amongst other things.'

'I don't know if I can go back on duty,' Alex replied, 'not after all this time.'

'Nobody's rushing you back to work,' McGovern said. 'Just take your time. We'll help you integrate back into the team in your own time.'

'Thank you, Neil,' Alex said to him. 'I also want

to use my married name, not my maiden name anymore.'

'Again, not a problem,' McGovern said.

Alex looked at Harry. 'Sorry, but I don't want that name now. I want to be Mrs McNeil, since we're married.'

'I'm glad.' Harry smiled at her.

'I have some work to do,' McGovern said, 'but you have Simon and Steffi's phone numbers. They'll be around for a little while, before their next assignment.'

With that, McGovern left the room.

'My head's spinning,' Alex said. 'I need a shower and to wash this hair dye out. Maybe go and get a proper haircut. The girl from McGovern's team is okay, but I'd like to get back to normality.'

'Me too,' Harry agreed.

'Neil said we can go to counselling, together and separately, and that's something I'd like to do.'

'We can do that.'

'Morgan was a psychiatrist, wasn't she?'

Harry felt a pain in his gut like he'd just been stabbed. He felt like he'd just been caught cheating. 'Yes, she was.'

Alex nodded, her thoughts staying in her head for the moment.

Harry wondered how Alex would have felt if Morgan was still alive, if she hadn't turned out the way she had. He wouldn't ask, not now, maybe not ever.

'Let's go back to the living room. Your little girl is waiting for you.'

FOUR

Detective Inspector Max Hold was just Max Hold this week. A vacation from the force, catching up with some old friends and having some fun while waiting for the finishing touches to be done on his new place.

Last night's fun had been in the local getting blootered, before staggering back to the boat with the help of...who? He didn't know, but he vaguely remembered it being a female. Whoever it had been, she had made sure he hadn't fallen into the marina and she hadn't nicked his wallet.

The coffee was good, but the hair of the dog was calling him. Nice sunny day, some tourists milling about, and he should be up and about. Right now, he was lying in bed, reading the news on his iPad...but then he heard shoes jump down onto his deck.

The tablet was tossed aside – carefully, he wasn't stupid – and he got out of his bed at the front of the boat and grabbed the tennis racket he kept at his bedside and opened the door silently. The boat gently rocked, but he was getting the hang of navigating through the vessel as it moved without falling over.

He walked from his bedroom into the main cabin and stopped to listen. The curtains were still closed on the small windows, so whoever it was on board, they didn't know he was on here.

The stairs leading up to the upper saloon were straight ahead behind a door. He walked forward and opened it. His friend who owned the yacht had told him the proper protocol was for a visitor to announce their presence, but so far nobody had.

He heard movement in the saloon above. He slowly went up the stairs.

'Bit hot for tennis, son,' an older man said. He had sat down on one of the benches at the table. 'I hope you don't mind, but I poured us a glass of orange juice since it's such a beautiful day. But by the looks of it, you need something a little stronger.'

Neil McGovern smiled at the detective as he approached.

'A phone call would have been appreciated,' Max said, putting the racket on the other bench.

'I did call. It went to voicemail.'

'Did it?' Max made a face and scratched his head.

'You had company round last night, I take it?'

McGovern looked at the man standing there in nothing but boxer shorts. The scars on his chest and upper arms were still evident from the job he had done for McGovern months ago. The weather had been very different back then, being in the grip of winter and the mission had left people dead, with Max barely escaping with his life.

'Maybe I should grab a t-shirt,' he said, then disappeared back down into the cabin below. He came back a few minutes later wearing cargo shorts and a t-shirt with the tour dates of a band from the '80s on the back and the artwork from one of their albums on the front.

'Genesis,' McGovern said. '*Invisible Touch.* Good album. Nineteen eighty-six, wasn't it?'

'It was. My old man saw them in concert in the Playhouse in nineteen ninety-two. You a fan?' Max sat down along from McGovern, his hair under control if not quite tamed. He drank some of the orange juice.

'I like them but prefer the Stones.'

'That's because you're older. They're a band for...'

'Old fogies like me?'

'People who prefer a more classic band.'

'I can see why you're so good in the interrogation room, son.'

Max drank some more of the cold juice. 'I didn't realise I had orange.'

'You didn't; I brought it with me. This is a nice boat.'

'I wish it was mine. My friend's coming up next week and he's going cruising somewhere in it. I think he should go to Spain.'

'I wouldn't even know how to start one of these things,' McGovern replied, 'never mind move it. But I'm sure Raymond doesn't have to worry about that when he pays somebody to move it for him.'

Raymond Mendoza was a very successful businessman who liked the finer things in life. He and Max had met years before at a party where Max was working undercover. He'd ended up saving Mendoza's life when the older man had gone into cardiac arrest. They'd stayed friends after that.

'He enjoys being able to sit back with his wife and let the staff do the hard work,' Max said.

'I'm sure Raymond could afford something a lot bigger than this.'

Max shrugged. 'Fifty-five foot isn't too bad.'

'True. I couldn't afford that on my salary.'

Max looked out at some of the other people going about their business on their boats. Most of them were sailing boats, and he couldn't even begin to imagine trying to get one of those moving.

'How's the house coming along?' McGovern asked.

'I decided on Anstruther.'

'I thought your old man came from Ballingry? That's where you were brought up, wasn't it?'

'It was, aye, but my auntie lived in Anstruther so I bought her house. It needed work done, but it's a great place. I've just got the finishing touches to do and then I can move in.'

'Good for you, son. God rest your auntie's soul.'

Max drank some more of the juice and put his glass on the table. 'Although I enjoy your company, Neil, I suspect you didn't drive over from Edinburgh for a wee chat.'

'Perceptive as ever. I have a wee job for you.' McGovern held up his hand. 'In exchange, I'll have a crew go into your auntie's house and finish it for you.'

Max made a face like he was deciding whether this was a good idea or not. 'I'm on holiday, but just for argument's sake, let's say I want this little job. Tell me what it is.'

McGovern's face was serious. 'Amy Dunn. Somebody murdered her.'

'What?' Max's face turned pale. 'How?'

'She was in the witness protection programme as you know. Yesterday, she was found dead at the Prince Albert memorial pyramid.'

'In the Cairngorms?'

'That's right, son. She was found by a couple of hikers, who have been eliminated as suspects already because of the time of death.'

'Isn't that a busy place for hikers in the summer?'

'Busy-ish. But this pair were the ones to report it. I want to know what she was doing up there and whether she was killed because of who she was.'

'Isn't Paul Hart in hospital?'

McGovern nodded. 'Yes, he is. He died this morning.'

'I'd read in the papers that he'd been ill for a long time,' Max said.

McGovern nodded. 'He was in the hospital a

few times. He'd been in the Royal under guard for the past week. He slipped away in the wee hours. Heart attack. It was his third, and this time it was fatal.'

'Coincidence?' Max asked.

'I don't know what it is. That's why I'd like you to go to Aberdeen.'

'Of course. Maybe give me a couple of hours to sober up a wee bit more.'

'No need. I have a driver for you.'

Max raised his eyebrows.

'Detective Sergeant Alex McNeil. She's been on secondment working for me for a while, and I asked her to do this job before returning to her team.'

Max looked out but couldn't see her and looked enquiringly at McGovern.

'She's waiting in the café. I told her you'd probably have been out on the lash last night, which is acceptable behaviour when you're on holiday, and she's okay with driving up north.'

'Right then, I'd better get ready.' Max stood up and looked at McGovern. 'How will I recognise her?'

McGovern stood up. 'You're the detective. You work it out. Keep in touch. And I meant what I said about having your place finished this week. They already started this morning.'

'That's very good of you, sir.'

'Don't thank me yet. You haven't seen their work. Catch you later, Max.'

McGovern walked out of the boat and along the gangway.

After a quick shower, drying hair that was cut short through choice not necessity to mask a receding hairline, Max dressed and walked along the gangway, feeling better physically, but mentally not so much.

There were several young women in the café, as well as what seemed like a coachload of men. To confuse him even further, three young women sat alone. *'You're the detective,'* McGovern had said. He tried to work out which one was DS McNeil. None of them were looking at him. One was reading a book, one was looking at some sort of chart thing and the third was writing in a notebook.

That had to be her, making notes for the journey. He approached her; she was young and slim and had dark hair. He looked for signs of a hidden weapon that she might be carrying; pepper spray, baton. Knife?

She looked up at him and smiled.

'Hi,' he said. 'I'm Max.'

'Hi,' the woman said.

'I was told you would be waiting for me.'

There was a slight shift in the woman's expression and he knew in that instant he'd got it wrong.

'Wrong table,' a voice behind him said. He turned to look at the woman closing the novel and standing up.

'Sorry,' Max said to the first woman. She smiled at him as if he was daft. 'I'm a police officer, here to meet somebody.'

That only served to make her think he was an escaped mental patient.

'He really is,' Alex said. 'He's a detective, believe it or not.'

The woman still wasn't convinced, but Max turned away from her in case she started asking questions, or summoned help.

'DS McNeil, I presume?'

'The one and only.' Alex held out her right hand to shake while keeping a grip on her hardback book.

'What are you reading?' Max asked her.

She looked down at the book for a second after they shook hands. '*How to Build Your Observation Skills*. I'll let you borrow it later.' She smiled at him.

'Neil said you were driving,' he said, changing the subject.

'The car's outside,' she said, holding her bible tight.

They walked towards the exit.

'Neil briefed you?' Max said.

'He did. He said you knew the victim years ago.'

They walked out into the sunshine, edged with a lick of wind coming off the water.

'I did,' Max replied, his mind going back to those days, picturing Amy's face. 'Amy was put into witness protection after giving evidence in a case against Paul Hart.'

'He died this morning,' Alex said.

'I know,' he replied as Alex stopped at a nondescript pool car.

'Now we're heading to Aberdeen.'

'We are,' Max confirmed. 'I'd also like to see the crime scene.' He looked at his watch. 'We're in for a long day.'

'Let's get started then.'

FIVE

Harry finished his coffee. Alex had left the house with Neil McGovern, and for a moment he had wondered once again if this was real. Had she really been home at all? He was disappointed that she felt like she couldn't come back to the team, but he didn't want to rush her. She'd been through a lot, being away from her baby and husband for the best part of a year, and it was going to take some adjustment to get back into the swing of things.

'It's going to be fine, Harry,' Jessica said to him. His sister-in-law had been a rock for him, and he was still leaning on her shoulder.

'I know it will.'

He was getting ready for work when his phone rang for the second time that morning. The first call had been to tell him that Paul Hart had died earlier that morning in the Royal Infirmary. Now Harry was wanted again.

He answered and listened to the caller before hanging up.

'Bad news?' Jessica asked, getting Grace ready for the nursery.

'Apparently, one of Paul Hart's cellmates wants to talk to one of us. Says he has some information.'

'That old line again.'

'Sometimes they have something useful, other times it's just a waste. But I'll go up to Saughton.'

'Have fun. I know *we* will.' She smiled at Grace before looking back at Harry. 'I know this is a transition period, with Alex being back, and I'll do whatever I can to help make it go smoothly.'

'I know.' He put a hand on her arm. 'I woke up this morning and thought I'd dreamt it all. Then Alex came out of her room, and although I saw her in the flesh, it still didn't seem real.'

'I know what you mean.'

'See you later,' Harry said.

'Not if I see you first.'

He smiled as he walked out into the warm morning. He got into his Jaguar F-Pace and drove down to the office at Fettes. Inside, it felt weird, thinking back to when he thought Alex was dead, knowing she had walked along these corridors, and now she would be walking them again.

He went into the incident room, where DI Charlie Skellett was sitting in front of a computer, banging away on the keyboard.

'Morning, Charlie. What's happening?'

Skellett stopped what he was doing and looked at his boss. 'I was just doing some background on Paul Hart, since he croaked it this morning.' He looked over at DS Lillian O'Shea, as if asking her to confirm that he could actually navigate his way around the computer without the aid of a hammer and swearing.

'We were just talking about him,' she said.

'I got a call telling me a cellmate of his wants to have a talk.' Harry looked around and saw DC Colin 'Elvis' Presley ducking down behind his computer screen.

'Elvis, you're up,' he said.

Elvis mumbled something in what sounded like a foreign language and then his head popped up, crumbs round his mouth. 'Coming, sir,' he said, washing his breakfast down.

'Sausage roll for breakfast? Manky bastard.'

'Sir Hugo loves a sausage roll for breakfast,' Skellett said, stopping clacking the keyboard for a minute.

'He's a dog, though,' Harry said. 'As long as Elvis doesn't start licking his arse.'

They all laughed, except Elvis. Then the door to the incident room opened and DI Frank Miller walked in with DS Julie Stott. If Harry hadn't known any better, he would have sworn the pair of them were seeing each other on the side.

'We're late because my car broke down and DI Miller offered to pick me up,' Julie said. 'Sorry about that.'

'It happens.' Harry looked across at Elvis. 'You finish your sausage roll, son. Frank, you're it. We're going to Saughton.'

'Okay.'

They were outside, walking to the car, when Miller looked at his boss and asked, 'How does it feel to have Alex back?'

'Strange as all hell, mate. Good, though, but it's going to take a wee while for it to seem real.'

'I have to admit, you could have wiped the floor with me when you phoned to tell me.'

'Kim's old man works in a department with secrets. He looked after her well with his team. Simon Gregg and Steffi Walker make a good team.'

They got in the car and Harry turned on the air conditioning.

'What will Neil do about the gravestone?' Miller asked as Harry headed out to Comely Bank.

'He said it's already been taken down. The empty coffin's been removed and we won't even think the ground's been disturbed, he says.'

'When I go down to Carol's grave again, I'll have a look,' Miller said.

'You still go down there?' Harry asked.

Miller nodded. 'I do. I can't get it out of my head, Harry. I'm married to Kim, I have a daughter and a stepdaughter, but I feel a sense of guilt that I've somehow left Carol there in the ground.' He looked out the window. 'Her and my unborn son.'

'You could always get help, pal. Help you move on. I'm not one to say how long to grieve, but it's been years.' Harry quickly looked at Miller. 'Can I ask you: are you having problems with Kim?'

Miller looked back at him. 'That's the thing; we're great. She works with her dad now, and she loves her job. I'm happy at work. I don't know what the hell's going on.'

They drove over Ravelston, heading up to Saughton. At the prison, they went inside and were shown into a room, where they waited. A guard brought a big man in and he sat down opposite the two detectives.

'Kenny Hughes,' Harry said. 'You requested an interview with detectives. The show's all yours.'

Hughes was twenty-nine, according to the profile Harry had been sent. Six foot four, sentenced to seven years for aggravated assault.

'Listen, I'm no' a pervert serial killer like Hart was. Smarmy bastard. I wanted to punch his teeth down his throat, but I also want to get out of here, so I kept my hands to myself. We spent a short time in the same cell. And that boy liked to talk. I think he was winding me up, like I would smack the shite out of him, but I ignored him. I want to get out one day to see my wee laddie. Know what I mean?'

Both men nodded in agreement that this was a reasonable way to think.

'Did he tell you anything that you think we didn't know?' Harry asked.

'The more he talked, the more I wanted to scud the fucker, let me tell you. Aye, he was talking a'right. Talking about killing more women than you lot knew about.'

Harry looked quickly at Miller before staring straight at Hughes. 'Any names?'

'Helen Hunt. She was killed when he was

younger, he said. I remember it because it was the same name as that actress lassie's. He said he killed her and buried her in a garden. Before he moved to London.'

'We have the names of his victims, including the ones who were dug up in his back garden,' Miller said, 'and Helen Hunt isn't one of them.'

'I don't know where he lived in Edinburgh before he moved south, but he said he met a woman down there and she became is girlfriend after he split with his wife.'

'Why didn't his girlfriend come forward and tell the police?' Harry asked.

'Did his wife come forward at first? The answer is no. Maybe she didn't know about it, but it doesn't alter the fact that this is what he told me. I know it's hearsay, but I'm sure you would rather know about it than not.'

'We would. Can you tell us any more details?' Miller asked.

'He just said he killed her before going back to his wife.'

'Anything else?' Harry asked.

'He mentioned another woman, a victim. He said she was a redhead. Older woman.'

'What was her name?'

'Rose, he said.'

'Was she killed in London?' Miller asked.

'He didn't say. He just described her and how she died. I warned him well: come near me and I'll snap your fucking neck. He left me alone, but he wouldn't shut up about how he killed the women. And this redhead, he said he had something special for her; he said he tortured her before almost strangling her, then just before she died, he stabbed her in the heart. Sick bastard.'

'Did he say where he disposed of the body?' Harry asked.

Hughes sat back in the chair. 'No. He just said how he killed them. He told me he had killed another forty-odd women in his time. He started when he was thirteen and he pushed his sister off a bridge. He told the police they were swinging on a rope that was tied to the girders and they were climbing up to it when she slipped and fell. He watched as she hit the concrete pier at the bottom on the water's edge. His sister's nickname was Angel, he said, because she was so heavenly.' Hughes tutted and made a face.

Miller wrote in his notebook: *Check Rose and Angel. And Helen Hunt.*

'You're sure he said she was his sister?' Miller said.

'That was what he told me,' Hughes answered.

'The only problem there is, he didn't have a sister.' Miller looked straight at Hughes, but the man's expression didn't alter.

'Again, he rambled on and on. That was just one of his stories. I don't have a clue whether he was making it up or not. I just wanted you to know some of the things he told me.'

'What else do you remember?' Harry asked.

'He said something strange before he was taken away to the hospital the other day.'

Harry and Miller waited while Hughes looked them both in the eyes.

'He said, "My legacy lives on."'

Both detectives stood up.

'Thanks for your information, Mr Hughes,' Harry said.

'You'll have a word with the Crown Office?' Hughes said, moving forward.

'I'll see what I can do. It depends if any of this information is of any use to us. Or if you've been spouting a bag of fairy tales.'

'Oh, they're real alright. He's a madman. Or was. Nobody in here will miss him.'

Harry knocked on the door and the guards came in.

Outside in the car, Harry sat for a minute. 'Suppose he is telling the truth. Was Hart telling the truth or just fabricating?'

'The sister story was made up; we know that for sure,' Miller said.

'He was probably embellishing his stories. But you and I both interviewed him and we know he was holding things back. Waiting to see if he could strike some kind of deal, like, take me out of here for a day and I'll show you where a body is hidden, that sort of stuff.'

'The others are going through his background. Maybe something will jump out.'

Harry started the car and left the car park.

SIX

Alex drove over the Queensferry Crossing bridge for the second time in as many days, the first time as a passenger sitting next to Harry, going in the opposite direction. She had felt anger coursing through her at the unknown threat that had kept her away from her husband and child for the longest time, but now that the threat was over the anger was still lingering. Even DI Max Hold had started out annoying her by talking to the woman at the other table, but now she realised it wasn't his fault, and he seemed like a nice enough man.

'You lived on the boat for long?' she asked as she headed up the M90. It was a two-and-a-half-hour journey and she didn't want things to be awkward between them.

'A couple of weeks,' Max answered, pulling a packet of mints out of his pocket. He took one out and offered the pack to Alex.

'You saying I've got bad breath, sir?'

'What? No, of course –' He stopped when he saw her grinning.

'I'm fine, sir.'

'I was a wee bit rough this morning and now my mouth is dry again,' he said, putting the packet away.

'You like the boat?' Alex said.

'I do. It's not mine. It belongs to a friend. He's letting me live on it until I get my house finished. I'm supposed to be on holiday this week, but Neil asked me to do this for him.'

'And he'll have your house finished for you,' Alex said.

'That was the deal he offered.' Max yawned and looked at his watch. 'I should have still been contemplating getting up.'

'That's what holidays are for. I wouldn't know, personally; it's something talked about only in closed circles.'

Max laughed. 'I haven't had a proper holiday for years. When I worked in London, it would be, take a week off, spend it in the pub.'

Alex heard a bit of a mixture in his accent: Fifer with London English.

'How long were you down there?' she asked.

'Fifteen years.'

'What made you come back?'

He looked over at her for a minute. 'I didn't like the politics of policing down there. I mean, it's not much better up here, but at least I'm in an area I know.'

Alex sensed the answer was more fiction than truth but didn't press it.

'So, Max Hold. I've seen that name on a pump bottle of hairspray before.'

'And you wouldn't be the first one to tell me that. I don't use the stuff myself, of course, so I'll have to take your word for it.'

'I wonder where the name *Hold* originates from?' Alex asked.

'I think it's from the Vikings.'

'More like Anglo-Saxons,' Alex said with a grin.

'I can see you've done your research on me already.'

'I was bored waiting in the café. Neil had given me some background, but I had to play around on Google.'

'It's going to be a long drive to Aberdeen.' Max

reclined his seat a bit and closed his eyes. 'I'll tell you if I need you to stop for a toilet or coffee break.'

'Maybe we could find a coffee first, then the bathroom, in that order.'

'You'll go far, Sergeant McNeil.'

As they entered Aberdeen from the south, Max was snoring and drooling from the side of his mouth.

Alex navigated her way to Cornhill Road with the help of Google Maps and parked outside the mortuary car park. Max was still in Wonderland as she turned the engine off.

'Wakey-wakey, sleeping beauty,' she said, shaking his shoulder and passing him a packet of paper hankies from her pocket.

He looked confused for a minute and spotted the hankies. 'Naw. Tell me I haven't.'

'If this was a first date, I would say that we should just be friends and then I'd ghost you, but since it's a work trip, I have to indeed confirm that saliva has run down the side of your face. You were either asleep or you've had a stroke.'

'Jesus,' he said, setting the seat more upright and taking the hankies with a nod of thanks. He took one out and passed the packet back, wiping his face.

'We won't speak of this again,' he said, balling up the tissue and putting it into his pocket.

'We won't if you spring for lunch later.'

'I don't think you should be flirting with me since you're a married woman.'

'It's not flirting, sir, it's blackmail.'

Max shook his head. 'I don't know what's worse.' He looked at his watch. 'It is lunchtime, I suppose. Have you stopped at a McDonald's?'

'Mortuary,' she said, nodding through the windscreen.

'Work first, then a bite to eat before we head over to the pyramid.'

'Sounds good to me.'

They got out of the car and walked past the open black gates to the main door of the nondescript building. Inside, the smell of death being cleansed hit their nostrils.

'I have no doubt that whatever mortuary we went to in the world, we'd be met with a similar smell,' Max said.

'My husband hates the mortuary,' Alex told him. 'It's not the sight of dead bodies but this smell that makes him gag.'

'He has my sympathies.'

They were greeted by a technician and they showed their warrant cards and explained they had been sent by Edinburgh.

'We did get a phone call telling us to expect you,' said the young woman, who had introduced herself as Crystal. 'Do you want anything to drink before I take you through?'

'I'm fine, thanks,' Alex said.

'Me too,' Max said.

'You should replenish your bodily fluids after dribbling all over the car,' Alex said in a whisper as Crystal walked ahead of them.

'Just keep that thought in mind when we're hiking to the crime scene. It's forty-five minutes, uphill. Don't worry, though, I won't go too far ahead of you.'

'That's very noble, sir.'

'Don't mention it.'

They went into the autopsy suite, where they were met by a female pathologist, Dr Ruth Starrow, who was a few years older than Crystal. She smiled like she was genuinely pleased to see them. Beside her was a stick-thin man with a dark moustache, also thin, like he was a member of an '80s tribute band.

'DS Robertson, this is DI Hold and DS McNeil,' Starrow said.

'Pleased to meet you,' Robertson said.

'Likewise,' Max said. He reckoned the older man was kicking on fifty.

'It's not that often we get visitors from Edinburgh,' Ruth said. 'Not ones who want to come in here anyway. But let me show you our client.'

'After you, sir,' Robertson said to Max. 'I've already seen her.'

They walked back into the refrigeration area. Crystal had gone ahead and she pulled open one of the drawers to reveal a sheet-covered body lying on the shelf. As she pulled out the shelf, Robertson hung back, while Alex and Max stepped forward.

'What was the cause of death?' Max asked.

'She was stabbed through the back into her heart with a long, sharp, tapered object. Like an ice pick.'

The words hung there between the five people. Max looked down at Amy Dunn's face. Crystal pulled the sheet down further to reveal more stab marks, deep rents in her skin. The deepest one was across her throat.

'That one was done postmortem,' Ruth said. 'It looks to me like he stabbed her from behind with the ice pick and then stabbed her after she died.'

'At the scene?' Alex asked.

'Not where she was found, no. There's something else too. Amy was pregnant. Three months.'

Max raised his eyebrows in surprise.

Robertson moved forward a step. 'The forensic

team found blood in the woods off to one side. Like she was standing with somebody in there and he took her by surprise. Then she was dragged over to the cairn.'

Max nodded and Robertson took a step back, like he was saying, *My job here is done*.

'Do you have a time of death, Doctor?' Alex asked.

Ruth looked at her. 'She was found yesterday around noon, and I estimated her TOD at around six hours before that.'

'Any witnesses?' Max asked, turning back to look at Robertson.

'No, sir. Not that we've had come forward anyway, but we've launched an appeal.'

'I would have thought that if somebody other than the people who found her had seen something, they would have come forward by now,' Alex said.

'We both know how that goes nowadays: nobody wants to get involved,' Max said.

'True,' Alex replied.

'Thanks for that, Dr Starrow. Crystal,' Max said. 'Now I'd like to go and visit the crime scene. After we use your facilities.'

Crystal showed them the way, and a few minutes later they were ready to hit the road.

'You mind if I join you in your car?' Robertson asked. 'The pool car I was using has been choried by the drug squad.'

'Fine by me,' Max said. He looked at Alex, silently asking if she minded what may or may not turn out to be an old minger in the back of her car.

'I'm okay with that,' Alex said.

'How will you get back?' Max asked Robertson, indicating that he was only going to be stopping once at Aberdeen on his tour of Scotland.

'I'll cadge a lift with the forensics crew.'

'Fine then. McDonald's to grab a bite to eat, then we'll be on our way.'

'Right then, we should get going,' Alex said. 'It's a wee bit of a drive. I'm not hungry, but I'll take you to McDonald's first.'

'And you not having had your lunch, Rab, you'll be wasting away,' Starrow said with a hint of sarcasm.

'I could do with losing a few,' Robertson said.

'Cutting out a few pints a week might go a long way.'

'Let's not get carried away, Doc.' Robertson smiled at her as they left.

Rab Robertson. Max thought the name was

familiar but didn't want to question the DS in case it sparked a conversation about ancestry.

Crystal smiled as she saw them out.

'Did I mention I'm a nervous passenger?' Robertson said.

'Indeed you did not,' Alex said.

'Aye, well, around the city is fine, if I close my eyes. But on a long trip, I can't help feeling this is my last day on earth.'

'It might very well be if I see you reaching to grab the wheel,' Max said. 'You sure you don't have access to your own car?'

'Afraid not. The boss won't let me drive after the last accident.'

'I thought you said you wanted a lift because the drugs guys took your car.'

'They did. The boss was driving it.'

Max stopped at their car outside in the street. 'Let me get this right: you don't drive anymore, and when you're in somebody's car, you're not averse to taking a Benny?'

'Pretty much sums it up, sir.'

'Sit in the back.'

'Way ahead of you. I can shout out directions from the back,' Robertson said.

'Or I can just use Google Maps,' Alex said, smiling.

'They never had that in my day,' Robertson said. 'I might not have rolled the car down an embankment if I'd had it.'

They got in, and within a couple of minutes Robertson was back-seat driving to McDonald's.

SEVEN

Dr Finbar O'Toole was settling into his new job as a pathologist in Edinburgh. His wife, a GP, was still working in Glasgow, and he was living in a serviced apartment, but life could be worse.

He could still be working in the mortuary in Glasgow.

He was standing in Dr Kate Murphy's office and they were drinking coffee.

Finbar looked at his watch. 'They should be on their way now,' he said.

Kate nodded. The body of serial killer Paul Hart was being brought down from the Royal Infirmary for a postmortem. Standard procedure when a prisoner died.

'He was a right evil bastard,' Kate said, her English accent thick. 'I was down there when he was killing.'

'He bounced all over the place with his family, I read,' Finbar said, leaning against the window frame of the office.

'He did. Murdering young girls and women.' Kate shook her head.

One of the mortuary assistants, a young Polish woman nicknamed Sticks because she was a drummer in a band in her spare time, popped her head into the office. 'Excuse me, boss, but he's here.'

'Thanks, Sticks.'

Both doctors put their coffee mugs down and walked out of the office into the receiving area, where a van was backing in through the loading doors, letting some cool summer air in with it.

Gus Weaver, one of the other techs, jumped out of the driver's side and walked round to the back, where Sticks helped him unload the transportation coffin onto a gurney. He was an older bloke who had retired but then come back part time, but he was now mostly full time again as there was difficulty filling his position.

'Straight up to the autopsy suite, please,' Kate said. 'I'll call MIT and tell them we're ready.'

As the body was wheeled along to the lift, Kate went back into her office to make the phone call.

EIGHT

Detective Superintendent Calvin Stewart stood next to the bistro table set for two and looked out of the living room window, down at the Dean Bowling Club below. A pair of arms slipped round his waist and he felt a body being pressed up against him.

'What are you doing to me, woman?' he said, smiling. He turned to face DSup Lynn McKenzie.

'God, Calvin, I don't know what's happening to me. I feel like a teenager again.'

He laughed. 'Aye, well, I don't have the body of a teenager anymore. Or the stamina.'

'You're doing just fine.' She kissed him and stood back.

'People say that to learner drivers.'

Lynn laughed and let him go. Stewart picked up

his coffee mug and took another sip. Then his phone rang.

'Uh-oh, work?' Lynn asked.

Stewart looked at the screen. 'It is.' He answered the call and listened before hanging up again. 'I have to get going.'

'Instead of staying here and entertaining me all day?'

'Oh, Lynn, tempting as that may be, duty calls.'

She laughed. 'Luckily, I'm on holiday for a few days.'

'You're a wicked lassie, teasing me like that. But I'll be back tonight.'

'You got anything special going on?'

Stewart looked at her. 'You know that serial killer Paul Hart?'

'Of course I do.'

'He died in the Royal Infirmary in the early hours of this morning. He's been transferred to the city mortuary. I'm going across the road to grab one of the team, then I'm going along while they do the postmortem.'

'He died without revealing anything else about the murders he supposedly committed, didn't he? The ones he told his cell mate about.'

'You're right. I got a text from Harry McNeil; he

went to speak with Hart's cellmate. He said he had information for us, so hopefully he wasn't just talking through his arse.'

'Call me later if you like. I'm going to have a wander around the charity shops.'

'Will do.' He put his jacket on before giving her a kiss. 'Who knew, eh? You and me.'

'Love works in mysterious ways.' She blushed a little. 'Well, not love, but you know what I mean.'

He put a finger over her lips. 'Let's just say there's some magic there, eh?'

She smiled as he left the flat.

Stewart thought he should be driving something better than a mundane saloon, and promised himself he would take Lynn with him when he went car shopping. He drove to the lights and hung a left, heading for Fettes Station, a building that was once the HQ of Lothian and Borders Police before the unification kicked in.

Inside, the team were at their desks, all but Harry and Miller.

'Elvis, I can see the coffee machine, son, but it's

either deid or on strike. If it's the latter, make it work again.'

'Usual, sir?' Elvis said, getting up from his desk.

'It is indeed. In a disposable cup. I'm glad you've got a good memory, unlike Charlie-boy there, skulking about with his troosers round his ankles again.'

'You wish,' Skellett answered.

'Still got your wee claw?' Stewart asked.

Skellett waved the metal back-scratcher in the air.

'That needs to be incinerated.'

'Doc says my leg isn't going to get better any time soon.'

'Fucking quacks. They know fuck all.'

They talked about the state of the NHS, each of them having an opinion on how it was fucked.

Elvis came over with the coffee.

'Thanks, son.' Stewart turned to Skellett. 'We're going to the mortuary. Get yourself ready to leave.'

'When?'

'Now.'

'That's fine, but you'll need to drive.' Skellett patted his leg.

'Fuck's sake. You can see I'm drinking coffee, can't you?'

'Unless we have an automatic at our disposal, you'll have to drive.'

Stewart looked at Elvis. 'Grab your coat, son. This lazy old bastard would rather be chauffeur-driven.'

Elvis grabbed his jacket and put it on.

'Right, you lot keep digging away at Paul Hart's life. Every man and his dug thinks the old fucker killed more women, so let's go over everything we can find on him. I know it's all been done before, but somebody might have missed something.'

The others nodded as Skellett grabbed his walking stick and he and Elvis followed Stewart out.

'Mind and take it fucking easy,' Stewart said, putting his seat belt on in the front of the car. 'I don't want my short and curlies burnt off.'

'I'll try my best, sir,' Elvis said as Skellett was still struggling with his belt in the back.

'You look like you've got a fucking ferret down your troosers back there,' Stewart said as Elvis moved away.

'The bastard belt keeps jamming when I pull it out.'

'That's because you're a fat bastard. You know, you're the only one I know who locks the seat belt no matter what vehicle you're in.' Stewart tutted and drank more of his coffee.

'That was a turn-up for the books, that bastard Hart popping his clogs this morning,' Skellett said, giving up on the seat belt and lounging back in the seat.

'No' really. It was only a matter of time, since he'd been in a few times already,' Stewart said, flipping his visor down and trying to look at Skellett in the vanity mirror. 'I hope you've still got your skids on.'

'Of course I have. I bought some new knee braces. They're a lot more comfortable than the old ones.'

'That's good to hear. No' before fucking time, though. We were going to start calling you Yo-yo, your breeks were up and down that many times.'

'I told the wife to keep Sir Hugo away from my troosers. The dug slavering on them without me noticing before I come to work is all I need.'

'It wouldn't be the first time, right enough.'

'Here, remember that time in Govan when that lassie fell in the river and you had to wade in to get her?'

'Nope. I don't remember any such fucking river.'

'You took your troosers off because you didn't

want to get yours wet, and then a uniform came booting down, shouting like we were a couple of paedos?'

'That must have been some other joker you were working undercover with.'

'No, it was you. The lassie took one look at you and started screaming. That was a right to-do. I had to dry off in the back of the car while you drove.'

'Again, another geezer.'

Skellett started laughing. 'Those were the days.'

'Where's the fucking radio in this car?' Stewart said, poking and turning the knobs, but he couldn't find anything until Elvis reached over and pushed the volume control.

'If a song comes on and reminds you of taking your fucking troosers off in public, keep it to yourself,' Stewart warned Skellett.

The Bay City Rollers came on and Skellett started singing 'Bye Bye Baby'.

'We could drive somewhere quiet,' Stewart said to Elvis, 'and write in the report that he took a Benny and things took a turn. I'll back you up all the way that it was self-defence.'

'As much as I'd like to...' Elvis let the sentence trail off.

'Just wait until your next report, that's all I'm saying. And turn that fucking radio back off.'

'Aw, Mother of Christ,' Skellett said from the back.

'What is it now?' Stewart said.

'This piece of chewing gum's got stuck on my plate.'

'Plate?' Stewart said. 'I didn't know you had falsers.'

'Just the front ones. I chew a wee bit of gum and I'm usually careful and just chew with my back teeth, but the bastard's on my plate now.'

Skellett fiddled with his dentures and took the top plate out. 'Aw, God, look at it,' he said, sounding like an eighty-year-old woman. He began to pull the offending gum off the plastic.

'Fuck me, that's minging,' Stewart said. 'Put it back, for God's sake.'

'Is that what your girlfriend says to you?'

'I don't have a girlfriend just now,' Stewart replied.

'Really. Must be another Calvin Stewart I heard about.'

Stewart ignored him.

'I can't go about all day with a blob of gum hanging off my plate.' Skellett pulled the gum and got most of it off, peeling the holdouts with a fingernail.

'That explains a lot. The other day when you were talking, I saw a sheep dug duck down on the pavement. I thought there was something wrong with it, but it was only you whistling while you were talking.'

Skellett put his plate back in and opened the window to flick the little bits of chewing gum out. 'That's better.'

'You're giving us the fucking boak,' Stewart said, screwing his face up. 'Try and keep your teeth in at the mortuary. I know they see some nasty stuff there, but they haven't seen anything like that.'

Skellett chuckled as Elvis kept on driving.

NINE

'I need some advice, boss,' DS Robbie Evans said. DCI Jimmy Dunbar put his Costa Coffee cup in the cup holder as Evans steered the car through the quiet suburb.

'First piece of advice: don't chew gum while you're drinking coffee.' Dunbar wound the window down and managed to spit the chewing gum far enough out so it didn't bounce off the doorframe and come back in with a vengeance, like the last time.

'Somebody'll be walking their dog and get that gum on their shoe,' Evans complained.

'I don't walk Scooby round here, so I won't have to look out for it. That's the trouble with people nowadays, always got their eyes on a phone while they're walking.'

'But still, it's littering.'

Dunbar rolled his eyes. 'You want this advice or not?'

'Aye.'

'As long as it's nothing like, "Should I take my auntie to the dancing?"'

'Aw, come on now. She's older than my maw.'

'And?'

'Look, if you're going to take the piss...'

'Just ask me, before I die of boredom.'

'Vern's talking about taking our relationship to the next level.'

'What, doing it with the bedroom light on?'

'Oh, for God's sake,' Evans said.

'Okay, if it's not that, what's the next level in her eyes?'

'Marriage. Getting hitched. Took me completely by surprise. I don't know what to do.'

'How did it take you by surprise? I thought you were a psychic? That's what you said Vern could see in you.'

'These are powers you shouldn't mock.'

Dunbar laughed. 'It's not as if you can move furniture just by thinking about it. If that was the case, you could have done my son's removal for half the price he paid.'

'You know what I can see? You not getting a bloody invite.'

'So you've subconsciously accepted the idea that you're getting married. You just want me to reassure you that you're doing the right thing.'

'Do you think I am?' Evans asked. 'I mean, I told her I'd think about it, but she's been buying wedding magazines.'

'Only you'll know if you're doing the right thing. You'll feel it in your gut. You'll look at her and not feel panic, knowing she's the woman who'll be your partner for life. Or for however long she can put up with your pish.'

'Thanks, boss. I just needed that wee pep talk.'

'I don't want this to bite me in the arse years from now. You know, when she's tossing your skids out the window into your garden.'

'I mean, I'm almost certain I want to go through with it.'

Dunbar held up a hand. 'Unless you're a hundred per cent, stay single. Go your own way. I knew I wanted to marry Cathy. There was no question. If you're having doubts now, you'll end up divorced and it's going to cost you a lot of money.'

'I think I'm just nervous.'

'What's to be nervous about? Her finding your stash of scud mags under the bed?'

'They're yours, remember?'

'I'm past needing those, son. But are you feeling guilty about leaving your maw?'

'A wee bit. Ever since my old man died –'

'She'll be just fine. Have you ever considered the fact that she might be waiting for you to leave so she can let her hair down a bit? That she'll feel relaxed that she can go out on the randan without worrying about what you'll think?'

Evans stopped at a traffic light. 'She's not like that.'

'She is, Robbie. She called me a couple of weeks ago.'

Evans stared at him for a second. 'You pulling my chain, boss?'

'Naw, Robbie. She wants you to be happy, and she thinks she's holding you back. She wants to go out with her pals and not worry.'

'Huh. I never thought about that before.'

'If that makes you feel any better about getting married, you should think about it but take your maw out of the equation.'

Evans pulled away and turned left. 'Makes sense, I suppose.'

'It does. I wouldn't steer you wrong.'

'Cheers, boss.'

'Now keep your fucking eyes on the road and let me finish my coffee before we get to this house.'

Five minutes later they were pulling up outside a house in Wishaw, outside the East End of Glasgow. It was an end-of-terrace house with a slabbed parking area in front instead of grass. And it was for sale.

The detectives got out of the car. Dunbar looked at the driveway, which led through to the back, where an old wooden garage sat.

The front door of the house next door opened and an old man poked his head out. 'Can I help you?'

'You the owner?' Dunbar said, nodding towards the house.

The man glared at him as if they were debt collectors. 'Who wants to know?'

Dunbar took in a deep breath and let it out again, resetting the clock on his frustration. 'Police.' Dunbar moved towards him and the neighbour stepped outside and down the few steps.

'You're here about the time Hart lived in there, I take it,' the man said. 'I heard about him on the radio this morning.'

'We are. We just wanted to have a look around.'

'I don't think the estate agent will be happy about that.'

'We have a warrant,' Dunbar said, just as the police van pulled up behind their car and uniforms bailed out.

'Oh, well then, I suppose it won't matter a toss.'

Just then a woman walked up, huffing and puffing as if she'd been training for a 5K.

'Oh, you're here already,' she said. 'Martha McCallum. I'm the estate agent.' She blew out a breath. 'I thought you might have smashed the door in. The house is empty, as you'll see.'

'DCI Dunbar, DS Evans. It was me you spoke to on the phone earlier.'

Martha looked around at the other men and women, scepticism crossing her face. 'Of course. But allow me.' She stepped past them and climbed the three steps to the door and opened it.

'We have ground-penetrating radar coming,' Dunbar said. 'We're going to be here all day. Do you know if there's anything in the old garage?'

'It's empty. It's not locked. There's nothing to steal.'

A sergeant walked up to Dunbar. 'The equipment's on the way, sir.'

'Thanks. We'll have a quick look inside, since it's

empty. Wait until the machine comes, then start on the back.'

'Will do.'

'That's a good place to start,' the neighbour said.

'What's your name, sir?' Dunbar asked.

'Archie Black. I've lived here for a long time, and the worst neighbour we ever had was that Hart. Creepy as all hell. He was a builder, you know?'

'I know.'

'He would bring materials out of his van at all hours. Push a wheelbarrow up the side of his hoose in the middle of the night. He laid a wee patio at the back of the garage, as well as the big one. He would put a tarp up, just to keep the rain off, he said. And then we find out he buried bodies in his house in London. I'm willing to bet you'll find something here too.'

'Thanks for that, Mr Black.'

'Here, you take the keys,' Martha said to Dunbar. He nodded to the uniformed sergeant, who stepped forward to take them.

'He'll be here longer than us,' Dunbar said.

'Just lock up when you're done,' Martha said, then turned away and marched back down the road to her car.

'Let's have a wee look around here,' Dunbar said to Evans, leading the charge as they went inside.

It had clearly been decorated for selling, the smell of paint still in the air. It looked nice inside, and if you didn't know better, it would seem like the house had had an uneventful history.

'You think there could be somebody under the patio outside?' Evans asked.

'Calvin Stewart interviewed Hart back in the day, and even he felt an aura of horror around the man. Mind you, if Hart had started his pish with our Calvin, he would have had his balls booted off, but that's beside the point.'

They walked around, looking in cupboards, finding nothing, and then ventured upstairs.

Nothing in any of the rooms; then Dunbar stopped and looked at the attic hatch in the ceiling. 'Get yourself up there, Robbie.'

'I can't even reach the door,' Evans replied, looking at the ceiling.

'You can on your tiptoes.'

Evans tried but couldn't push the wooden door up.

'Go and get two uniforms. The biggest bastards down there.'

A few minutes later, two young officers came up

and Dunbar instructed them to lift Evans enough so that he could push the attic door. They grabbed a leg each and lifted him, and he pushed the door up and then took hold of the surround and hauled himself up.

'Thanks, lads,' Dunbar said as Evans brought his phone out and turned the light on.

'What do you see?' Dunbar shouted.

Evans walked further into the attic.

'Put gloves on, Robbie!' Dunbar reminded him.

'Aye-aye, Captain.'

Dunbar heard the distinctive snap of latex gloves being put on. Boots clumping on rafters, interspersed with swearing.

'See anything?' Dunbar shouted up.

'Aye, a light pull,' Evans shouted back down, and Dunbar saw the attic being illuminated, if not exactly flood-lit. 'Wait a minute.' The sound of more movement.

'What is it?' Dunbar said, impatience creeping into his voice.

'There's a cardboard box up here.'

'Fuck's sake, Robbie, can you be a bit more specific?'

'It has "Walkers Crisps" written on the side.'

'I meant, what's inside it?'

'I'm making my way over to it now, boss.' More clumping. 'Oh, ya bastard,' Evans shouted.

'What is it?' Dunbar shouted.

'I banged my heid.'

'I'll boot you in the fucking heid if you keep the shenanigans up.'

'Fucking place is stinking. Like my grannie's hoose.'

'Get a move on, for God's sake. If you find an axe murderer up there hiding, you're on your own, I hope you know that.'

'Och, away,' Evans answered. 'Oh Christ, there's a rat running towards the hatch.'

'You're the only fucking rat up there,' Dunbar said, but moved a couple of feet back just in case. When it was evident that no rodent – six foot or otherwise – was coming down, he moved back.

'Christ,' Evans said. 'There's things wrapped in newspapers here, boss.'

Dunbar waited for Evans to elaborate.

'Hey, boss!' Evans shouted, like he had indeed discovered an axe murderer lying in wait. 'Get forensics in here!'

'What have you found?' Dunbar shouted back.

More clumping of boots until Evans appeared at the hatch. 'You're never going to believe this.'

TEN

'Be on your best behaviour,' Stewart warned as they got out of the car at the mortuary in the Cowgate.

'Aye, Elvis. Mind your manners,' Skellett said.

Stewart looked at him. 'Don't make me give you a boot in the knackers.'

Elvis ignored them both as they walked towards the personnel door.

Sticks answered with a smile. 'Detective Calvin, big boy from Fettes.'

Stewart smiled at her. 'Morning, Sticks.' He held the door as she walked away.

'She must mean you're a fat bastard,' Skellett said in a low voice.

'I heard that,' Stewart said, letting the door go on the DI.

'God, I'm walking with a stick here,' Skellett complained.

'What am I, a fucking doorman?'

'Letting the door go on a disabled man. What next?'

'Just keep all your smelly wee scratching tools in your pocket. We're in company.'

Elvis closed the door behind them.

'I've lost count of how many times I've been in here,' Skellett said. 'Hey, boss, you remember that time we spent the night in the Glasgow mortuary?'

'I've never set foot in a mortuary before,' Stewart answered.

Skellett chuckled as he clunked along with his walking stick. 'When somebody comes out with pish like that, you know they're lying.'

'Do you think I'm lying, Elvis?' Stewart said, falling back a bit as they crossed the receiving area.

'I don't think you are, sir.'

'See? Now stop havering a load of pish.' Stewart carried on and caught up with Sticks. She was standing next to Gus Weaver, the older mortuary technician.

'Why did you say that?' Skellett asked the young DC.

'He has to write my annual report,' Elvis answered.

'Good choice. I would have done the same thing if I was in your shoes.'

Kate Murphy was waiting for them. 'Good morning, gentlemen. Finbar's upstairs, waiting for us.'

'Morning, Kate,' Stewart said. He knew the death of her partner, DS Andy Watt, was still raw, so he made an effort to skirt round it.

'This day couldn't come quickly enough,' Skellett said. 'That bastard should be burning in hell by now.'

'I'm sure he is, but his body is waiting for us to examine,' Kate said.

They all made their way up in the lift to the autopsy suite, where Finbar O'Toole was already scrubbed up.

The detectives put on protective gear.

'Hi, Fin, how's tricks?'

'Good to be back working with the dead, I have to admit,' Finbar said, smiling.

'I'll deal with the living and you deal with the dead, and we'll meet somewhere in the middle, eh?' Stewart said.

'Aye, sounds about right.'

Paul Hart lay on the stainless-steel table, old and

shrivelled. Looking at his body, nobody would have believed the evil the man had been capable of, but all of them in the room knew exactly what this man had been like.

Sticks and Weaver had their protective gear on. Weaver began cutting open Hart's skull to remove the brain for weighing. He removed it and handed it to Sticks, who put it on the scales. After the weight was recorded, Kate made the incision and they all watched her open Hart up.

'Harry McNeil would be shitting himself by now,' Stewart said, grinning. 'He's one of the best, but by God does he hate the smell of this place.'

'Mind you once puked at a crime scene,' Skellett said.

'That's enough of that talk now, Charlie. I'm sure you're mixing me up with somebody else.'

Stewart looked at him, silently promising him he'd be the next one on the table if he didn't curb his enthusiasm. Skellett shrugged.

The stomach was taken out and weighed and the contents examined in a bowl.

'What's this?' Kate said. She carefully lifted out what looked like a very pale, limp sausage.

'A condom,' Elvis said, like he was a contestant on a TV show.

'Are you going to be blurting things out willy-nilly, son?' Stewart said.

'Sorry, sir.'

'Carry on, Doctor,' Stewart said.

Kate took a scalpel and held the condom with a pair of surgical tweezers and careful cut it open. Then she grabbed the contents with another pair of tweezers.

'It's a piece of paper,' she said, and everybody in the room watched as she unrolled it and read the writing on it.

This isn't over.

ELEVEN

There was a group of hikers waiting down near the distillery, eager to wander about, but they were being held back by uniformed officers. Alex parked behind a van and waited a second for Robertson to wake up.

'Are we there yet?' Robertson asked.

'Yes,' Max said.

'I was just closing my eyes against the glare,' Robertson explained. 'I forgot my sunglasses.'

They got out of the car and showed the uniform standing guard their warrant cards. They were let through and were shown the direction to take.

Another uniform came over with three bottles of water. 'It's a bitch of a climb,' he said.

Alex and Max looked at Robertson for confirmation. The older detective nodded.

'Bitch,' he confirmed. 'Come on, I'll show you.' Robertson started off ahead of them.

Alex and Max followed. The trees afforded them some shade, but the ground was rough on their feet and the incline rough on their knees.

Alex pulled ahead, digging deep, and she didn't feel the climb was too bad. Max, however, looked like he was going to cough up a lung when he got to the top. He was sweating and his face had turned red.

'Oh, sorry, sir, did you want me to let you win the race to the top?' Alex said, smiling.

'I just let you get ahead while I stopped to take in the views,' he said, bending over, putting his hands on his knees and trying not to share his lunch with the Highland cows he was sure were lurking around somewhere.

They broke through the trees into a clearing, with the pyramid in front of them.

'That's huge,' Alex said.

There was yellow crime-scene tape tied to a tree and to a pole on the other end. A forensics tent had been placed to one side, presumably to cover the victim while she was there.

'I think Robertson must have ducked into the woods for a pee or something,' Max said. 'I didn't see him on the way up.'

'There, he's over there, talking to one of the forensics team.'

'He's not even sweating. Did he get a helicopter up here?'

White-suited forensics officers were floating about and one of them came over. 'Help you?' she said.

'DI Max Hold. DS Alex McNeil. We're from Fife. The victim came from there, so we've been involved.'

'Tasha Moran. Over this way.' The woman smiled and pulled back her hood. She was dark skinned and a veil of sweat covered her forehead.

'That's some walk,' Alex said. 'You must be roasting in that suit.'

'Almost done now. We've searched and photographed and documented everything. I'll show you where she was found.' Tasha led them into the tent, which afforded them some relief from the sun beating down overhead.

There was still blood on the stone.

'She was killed in the woods,' Tasha explained. 'There was a lot of blood over there. Then she was carried here; there's no evidence of her being dragged. Whoever did it must have been covered in blood. That's why he burnt his clothes further into the woods. Luckily, he didn't burn the whole place down. He was very careful, and very methodical. I assume he just burnt a little bit of his clothes at a time, so as not to create a huge fire and attract attention. There's evidence of a pair of jeans, underwear, socks and a shirt.'

'He must have been carrying a backpack with a change of clothes,' Alex said.

'I would assume that. Better to not attract attention by walking about nude, especially near the castle,' Robertson said.

Max nodded and looked at the man. Not a bloody bit of sweat on him. 'It seems she was stabbed through the back into her heart, possibly with an ice pick, then she was stabbed again after that.'

'That would make sense,' Tasha said.

'He would probably have been wanting to keep cover until the last minute,' Alex said.

'It was risky, though,' Max said. Then he looked at Tasha. 'We were at the mortuary and spoke to the pathologist, and she estimated time of death at six hours before discovery, which would mean he killed her early morning. When it would have been light.'

'Maybe he figured nobody in their right mind would be thumping up the hillside that early in the morning,' Alex said.

'We'll be wanting to see the photos of the victim as she was here,' Max said to Tasha.

'No problem. She was sitting up against the stone. You know, leaning back, like, but in a sitting position.'

'What was she wearing?'

'Shirt, shorts and hiking boots. A light jacket,' Robertson said.

'Did she have a purse on her?' Max asked.

'Yes. There was money in it,' Tasha said. 'It had some cash, credit cards and a note.'

'A note?' Alex said.

'Yes. A piece of paper, folded, in beside the bank notes,' Tasha said.

'Do you remember what it said?'

'Yes, it was strange. "Me and all the others."'

'Could mean anything,' Alex said.

Max nodded, not wanting to say any more. He was convinced that Amy Dunn was a victim of Paul Hart's, whether he was dead or not.

TWELVE

1980

'Go and get your sister.' The boy's mother stood looking at him. 'Tell her she's late. Lunch was ten minutes ago.'

'Do I have to?' The boy made a face.

'Please, little man. She'll come in and whine about how she didn't have any lunch and how she's starving and it's all my fault, and she'll go off her head again.'

'Okay, Mum,' the boy said.

'It's twenty to one. She should have been here ten minutes ago, but she doesn't listen.'

'I said I'll go, Mum.'

'She'll probably be in the park again, hanging out with God knows who.'

'I'll go and tell her, but I can't make her come back. I don't want to set her off again.'

'Thank you. You're such a sweet boy. I wish I had two kids like you.'

'Don't say that too loudly.'

The boy left the house, which was in Redbraes, a part of Bonnington. He walked through the park, towards the railway line, and crossed the small bridge that spanned the Water of Leith, then headed up into St Marks Park, walking adjacent to the river, the Powderhall refuse depot on the opposite side. Long grass grew on the embankment on both sides of the river. He looked at the footbridge in the distance, the iron girders holding up the wooden planks.

But it was the girl swinging out on the rope from underneath the bridge that caught his attention.

His sister.

He felt a mixture of fear and dread. Her smile could change in an instant from one of innocence to that of somebody possessed.

He scuttled down the side of the steep embankment. Opposite was a sluice that sloped down from the refuge depot into the water. His sister saw him while she was at the end of the arc, holding on to the rope for dear life. She had obviously taken off from a point on the embankment up from the river. There were knots on the rope; the higher up the knot, the higher up the embankment you had to be to swing out.

She dragged her feet to a stop, kicking up dust.

'You want a shot?' she asked.

'No. Mum said to come and get you for lunch.'

'What? I'm not hungry.'

'I'm just the messenger.'

'Well, here's a message: tell her to go and piss off. I'm having fun and I'll be home when I want to be.'

Although he was thirteen now and not a daft twelve-year-old, she was still sixteen, bigger and heavier and certainly meaner. And harder, if truth be told, although he wouldn't admit that to his pals.

'Okay. I'll tell her you're playing.' He was about to turn away when she laughed.

'You're scared,' she said, swinging out again.

'Of what?'

'Of this rope. I bet you wouldn't climb up the girders and swing from the top.'

'I would. Of course I would.'

'Go on then, show me,' she said, dragging her feet to brake again.

'I'm going home for lunch,' the boy replied.

'You're just a wee fanny.'

'No, I'm not, ya boot.'

The repercussion from his insult was so swift, he didn't really see it coming, but he should have. He was prepared on a daily basis. Prepared for the onslaught of her streak of violence directed towards him and his mother.

She punched him in the stomach, and as he bent over, she grabbed his hair and pulled.

'I told you before not to call me names, you little bastard,' she said.

When she let him go, he could see the spittle on her lips and the fire in her eyes.

'Sorry,' he said, trying to get his breath back. 'I didn't mean it.'

'That's okay,' she said, the smile back. 'Just don't do it again.'

He stood there for a full five minutes, getting his breath back and rubbing a hand over his hair, hoping it looked close to how it had looked before he left the house.

He made his way back up the embankment, expecting to hear her shout, but nothing came. Back up in the park, he retraced his steps.

He didn't see the man sitting in the long grass that bordered the park.

'That was something to see,' the man said, and the boy could only see the wisp of cigarette smoke rising above the long stems of grass. Then the man sat up and he could see him from the waist up. He was young and had thick black hair and a nice smile.

The boy was scared at first and was like a hare waiting to run.

'Smoke?' the man asked.

'Nope.'

'You should have hit her back, you know,' the man said, taking another drag on his cigarette.

'I don't hit girls,' the boy said.

'And you shouldn't. That's not a nice thing to do. But she's older than you, and bigger and stronger. It's called self-defence. It's not as if you'd be picking on the girl.'

'She's my sister.'

'Ah. That makes it alright. Until one day when she picks up a knife and stabs you to death with it.'

'She wouldn't do that.'

'I'm glad you're confident. But I saw the way she twisted her face as well as her hands; the anger in her face was unmistakable.'

'Who are you?' the boy asked.

'That doesn't matter. What matters is, are you going to let her get away with hurting you like that? Until one day she kills you.'

'She won't kill me.'

The young man smiled and drew on his cigarette again. 'I'm glad you're so sure. But I've seen it before. Then they start saying how sorry they are, how they didn't mean it, and they cry in court.'

'Are you a policeman?'

The man laughed. 'No, I'm not a policeman. I'm just somebody who's met people like your sister before, that's all. And they don't stop. They get their own way. You know what somebody like your sister is called?'

The boy shook his head.

'A narcissist. Somebody who is only interested in themselves. If she killed you, she would manipulate anybody who got in her face. She would turn things around so that it was all your fault, and you wouldn't be here to defend yourself.' He took a last drag and nipped the cigarette, careful not to throw it away into the grass and cause a fire. 'Let me ask you something: how many times has she hit you in the past?'

The boy shrugged. 'Loads. Me and my mum.'

The young man raised his eyebrows. 'Your mum too? That takes things to a whole new level. I now have no doubt in my mind that she would kill you and your mum if she got the chance.' He stood up.

They both looked over as the boy's sister

squealed and she sailed out over the river, gripping the rope as if her life depended on it.

The young man stepped closer to the boy, his jeans rustling the grass. 'You could make it look like an accident.'

The boy looked at him for a moment. 'What do you mean?'

'You wouldn't miss your sister if she was gone. I should know; my sister had an accident. After she told me she was going to kill me.'

'I...I can't do that.'

'You can. If you really want to. Just think back to the last time she hit you. The time before today, I mean. How did you feel? Hopeless? Powerless? Angry? Scared? Were you able to fight her off? I don't think you were, from what I just saw. Tell me, how would you feel if you could walk into your house every day and know you weren't going to get a kicking?

'The kind of anger I've just seen gets worse and worse. She'll hurt you more and more, and it will never stop. The pain will be excruciating. You won't be able to stand it...until she lets you go and you look down and there's a knife sticking out of your belly. She might put a knife in your hand as you lie on the kitchen floor, dying. She'll tell the police that you went on the rampage. If your mother is in, she might kill her too. Blame it all on you. Because you'll have the knife in your cold, dead hand. And she'll walk away laughing.'

The boy's mouth was dry and he felt dizzy. He couldn't imagine life without his mum. The last time his sister had beaten them, he had thought she was going to kill his mum because the punches were so fast and hard.

'How...how would I...?' He couldn't believe the words were coming out.

'I'll tell you. It will be easy. You might feel panic to begin with, but trust me, it will pass. And you just need to keep your story straight and nobody will think anything else.'

The man stepped closer and told the boy what he needed to do.

The boy walked away, back towards the bridge. Scrabbled back down the embankment. He looked back over to where the man was and could just make out the green shirt in the tall grass because he knew the man was there. Somebody looking casually across wouldn't see him.

'I'll do it,' the boy said to his sister as she came screaming back in.

'Do what?'

'I'll swing from the top girder if you'll do it first. Show me what to do.'

His sister laughed. 'Come on then, but hear this: if you don't do it, I'll put the rope round your neck and throw you off.'

If there were any lingering doubts at that point, they vanished in an instant.

They climbed up the iron girders, putting their hands and feet in the holes in the metal, using them as ladders. The boy carried the rope over his shoulder, tilting his head at times when he thought it was going to fall off, securing it with his neck.

When they were at the top, the height looked frightening.

'Have you done this before?' he asked.

'Of course I have. It's fun. You sail out and you think you'll come back and hit the bridge, but you don't. But you see the rope doesn't quite reach, so you have to get somebody to hold it for you while you jump and grab it near a knot. That's why I had you put it over your shoulder. Now, wait until I'm in position, then hold on with one hand and hold the rope out with the other.'

'Like this?' he said, holding the rope out while holding on for dear life with the other hand, the iron column cold in his hand. He focused on the grey paint chipping away, not looking at her.

'Are you ready?' she said, grinning at him.

He nodded. 'Yes.'

'It's now or never at this point,' his sister said, the last words she would ever utter to him.

From her perch on the girder, she let go, both hands reaching out for the rope, and just before she could grab it, he pulled the rope sideways, away from her.

She looked at him then, just for a split-second, and if truth be told, he would see that face in his dreams for years to come.

There was a short scream as she sailed out into thin air, her hands grabbing nothing, and then she hit the dry, hard riverbank, head first. The crack was audible from his perch, and he thought he was going to be sick, but he didn't – he let the rope go and it swung out on its own, and he scrambled along the girder. It was high, but he managed to climb out onto the side and up, then he carefully stepped along.

This was the point where if there were any witnesses, he would say that they had been playing with the rope and his sister had fallen. The result might have been his mother blaming *him*, telling him he shouldn't have encouraged her, or he should have been more careful, but there was nobody there. He was on the side of the refuge depot, so if anybody had been looking out of their windows from the houses in Warriston Road, they wouldn't have been able to see him clearly.

When he was back on the grass, there was nobody on the path. He hurried along and saw the young man standing by the pathway that led back to the railway tracks.

'You did well. You've only been a few minutes. Your mother might wonder where you've been, but you say you didn't see anybody on the rope, it was just hanging there, so you looked about the park for a minute and couldn't see her. You stick with that and nobody will blame you.'

'I killed her,' the boy said, panic gripping him now.

'She fell. I saw you. If this ever goes sideways, I'll come forward as a witness and say that I was walking and saw you and you never went near the rope.'

'She's dead. I saw her lying there.'

'You'll never have to worry about her hurting you again.'

The boy looked at the man. 'What's your name?'

'That's not important just now. I'll see you again, though. Don't look for me. I'll find you.'

They walked down the pathway to the railway tracks. The boy went back the way he had come and the young man walked along the pathway in the opposite direction.

When the boy looked from the railway bridge, there was no sign of the man.

THIRTEEN

Present day

'Hart's next of kin have been told, but they don't want anything to do with him,' Harry said, standing at the whiteboard. 'His wife died years ago and his two daughters washed their hands of him. They won't even acknowledge he was their father.'

Calvin Stewart was sitting with his feet up on a desk. 'I don't blame them,' he said. 'I mean, my old man wasn't up for the Parent of the Year award, but at least he didn't go about hammering young lassies. I don't blame Hart's daughters.'

Charlie Skellett had his claw back-scratcher out

and was scratching the back of his leg at the top of his knee brace. 'Fucking thing.'

'Why don't you just keep it off?' Stewart said, turning his nose up.

'My leg buckles and I don't want to take a heider going down a flight of stairs.'

'Might knock some sense into you. But carry on, Harry, son.'

'I just want to talk about the elephant in the room for a minute, sir, if that's okay.'

'That's no way to talk about Charlie.'

'Funny,' Skellett said, waving his claw in Stewart's direction.

'If that thing fucking touches me...'

Skellett laughed and looked at Harry. 'Sorry, sir.'

'No problem. This is difficult, but since you're all here, I'd like to talk about it for a minute. My wife, Alex. I've only discussed this with DSup Stewart and DI Miller before now, but I think you should know. It turns out that my wife wasn't dead at all.'

There was a murmur in the room for a second before Harry held up his hand. 'It's come as a shock to me too, believe me. She was in protective custody. There was intel that somebody wanted us dead, and it was arranged that Alex had to be taken out of the picture. It was a huge sacrifice, but she wanted to protect our daughter. If they thought she was dead, that would divert their attention onto me. It turns out that Grace was still in danger, but that threat was neutralised, as you all know.

'I wanted to tell you before now, but I was advised not to until I spoke to Alex. She doesn't want to come back to the team right away, which is fine, as there isn't an opening for her. She's working with a DI in Fife for the moment, and they're investigating the murder of a young woman who was in the witness protection programme. She was found killed at the Prince Albert memorial cairn in the Cairngorms. Alex will be working with DI Max Hold for the time being, looking into Amy Dunn's background to see if her murder is connected to Paul Hart.'

'Why would we think it's connected?' Frank Miller asked.

'Amy Dunn used to go by another name back in the day, when she was a witness for the Crown Prosecution Service in London. She helped put Paul Hart away. Then she was transferred to Fife. And the connection would fit in with a couple of notes that were found. One of them in Amy's purse. It read, "Me and all the others."'

'That could suggest that she was a victim, just like all of Hart's other victims,' Stewart said.

'Except she wasn't a victim of Hart,' Harry said. 'Not exactly. Max Hold said that the pathologist puts her time of death at around six in the morning. Paul Hart died at two fifteen in the morning. In the Royal Infirmary. So obviously he wasn't the killer.'

Stewart put his feet down. 'And Hart had a condom in his stomach with a note in it. It said, "This isn't over."'

'He obviously knew Amy Dunn was about to be murdered,' Skellett said.

'I think he knew he was on his last legs,' Miller said. 'We all know that things are easily smuggled into prison. Including condoms, obviously. Hart must have swallowed one when he was in his cell, knowing he didn't have much chance of making it out of the Royal, and if he did, he would just pass it through and start again.'

'Unless he swallowed it in the hospital,' Elvis said. 'Which would mean he needed somebody to give it to him, and since we know somebody else killed Amy Dunn, could it be the killer who's working with him who passed Hart the condom?'

'Good thinking, Elvis,' Harry said.

'Those messages,' Lillian said, '"This isn't over" and "Me and all the others", suggest that Paul Hart wasn't working alone. At least now he isn't. Maybe years ago, but now he has somebody else to carry the torch.'

'That would make a lot of sense,' Stewart said. 'Hart's last heart attack was fatal, but by all accounts he was admitted to the hospital with a lesser heart attack. He knew he was in poor health and that he might indeed die, either in prison or the hospital, so at some point he swallowed the condom. He knew if he died, the message would be found in his stomach. He wanted to go out on a high, which was sticking it up us. Letting us know that even though he's dead, somebody else out there is carrying on for him.'

'Or we could be jumping the gun here entirely,' Julie said. 'What if Amy Dunn was killed by some-body else not connected to Hart? Yes, there was a note in her purse, but what if this has nothing to do with Hart?'

'It's an avenue we're exploring, Julie,' Harry said. 'We don't want to be chasing our tails, so we're keeping an open mind on the connection, but we can't rule it out.'

'I also got a call from Jimmy Dunbar in Glasgow,' Stewart said. 'They were checking out an old address of Hart's, through in Wishaw. It's empty and up for sale. Up in the attic was a box with what can only be described as "trophies" in it. From Hart's victims, or what we believe to be Hart's victims. There was a photograph in a frame of Wilma Fletcher. She went missing in Wishaw back in nineteen ninety-six. This isn't one of her family's photos, but one cut from a newspaper and put in a frame.'

'That's the first time I've ever heard of that happening,' Harry said.

'Me too. And there were two more frames, each with a newspaper clipping photo in it. One of Pamela Grant and the other of Heather Thomas. Pamela went missing in the Livingston area in the nineties, Heather from Dunfermline train station in the late nineties. None of the women have been found. But here's the twist: the photo frames were wrapped in newspaper dated last Monday. Somebody put them up there within the last week or so.'

'It wasn't Hart,' Skellett said, 'playing into our theory that he has somebody working for him.'

'There was one more thing,' Stewart said, 'an old newspaper clipping with a review for the film *Twister* with the actress Helen Hunt on it.'

'That was a name Hughes told us in Saughton,' Harry said.

'So you said. The thing is, there's no Helen Hunt listed as a missing person,' Stewart said.

'We checked for missing females today,' Lillian

said. 'There's no Helen Hunt on the list, but there is a young woman called Helen Marsh. Reported missing a couple of days ago by her husband.'

Harry looked at her. 'Whereabouts?'

'She lives over in Dalgety Bay.'

'I'll have a word with Hold tomorrow and see if he can have a talk with the husband. Leave the address out.'

'Will do.'

'I have to admit I'm still in disbelief about Alex.'

'You and me both, sir.'

'Aye, it's going to take a wee bit of adjustment, that,' Skellett said. 'I don't envy you, but wish you all the best. Hopefully, those of us who haven't met Alex can meet her soon.'

'I'm sure she'd like to get to know you all better in the boozer, Charlie,' Stewart said. 'Although she's probably heard of you. The name Charlie Skellett is spoken only in certain circles, usually when the younger ranks are blootered and say things like, "Can you believe that old bastard Charlie Skellett isnae deid?"'

'Some legends are merely myths, but here we are, I'm living and breathing as we speak,' Skellett said, grinning. 'Now, if you'll excuse me, I have to go and put powder on my knee.'

'We're finished here for the day anyway,' Stewart said. 'Back here nine sharp tomorrow.'

'We can be in at eight, sir,' Harry said to Stewart as the others were busy getting themselves ready to leave.

'This is going to be a tough case, Harry, son. Nine is fine.'

When Harry looked around for Frank Miller, he was surprised to see that the DI had already left.

He packed up for the night and wondered for the first time in a very long time whether his wife would be home in time for tea.

FOURTEEN

Frank Miller stopped into the Waitrose next to the station, picking up a carton of orange juice, bread and a bouquet of flowers. The first two were items that his wife had asked him to pick up. The third was an impulse buy. And not for his wife.

Not his second wife. Sure, he bought Kim flowers on a frequent basis, but today they were for somebody else.

He drove up to Warriston Cemetery again. Recently, he had been visiting here, each time bringing a bunch of flowers but not writing a card. He didn't have to write a card. Carol would know who they were from.

It was still warm outside, the sun making the cemetery a pleasant place to be.

He parked on the track and walked over to the gravestone in the new part. He could walk through here blindfolded, he'd been here so many times.

He read the inscription: Carol Miller. And their unborn son, Harry. He stepped forward and laid the flowers on her grave and felt the sadness grip him inside. He missed Carol so much, and often wondered what direction his life would have taken if she hadn't died that night.

He loved Kim, he loved her daughter and he loved his own daughter; that wasn't in question. But Carol had been taken away from him suddenly.

Miller had felt empathy for Harry McNeil when Alex had died. It had been shocking for them all. Now he had her back. Miller felt envious. Glad his friend had his wife back with him, of course, but Miller wished that he could have his Carol back.

'I got these for you, sweetheart,' he said, putting the flowers down on her grave. 'The weather's been mixed these past couple of weeks.'

Jesus. Was that the extent of his conversation nowadays? The weather?

'Remember when we went to Colin's party? At New Year? That was a laugh. My dad got blootered and we had to pile him into a taxi. My mum was furious, but we had a good laugh. I miss those days. I wish we could celebrate again. Harry's a lucky man having Alex back. Don't get me wrong, she's a nice lassie, and I'm glad she's back, but it just seems so surreal. Here Harry is, grieving his loss, moving on with another woman, and then she dies and his wife comes back to him. He loves her more than anything. I wish him all the best, but I can't help wishing it was you.'

He stood up straight and read her name a couple of times more.

'I'll see you soon, sweetheart.'

He turned and walked away, back to his car. He had been coming to Carol's grave for months now, laying flowers at Christmas and any other time he wanted to come. Like just now.

Of course he didn't tell Kim. How could he? How would he explain it away? He would have to admit to her that he had been eavesdropping on her and her dad one evening when he had come home from the pub early. They clearly hadn't heard him coming in. He had been quiet because he didn't want to wake up the bairns, and he had heard them talking.

Talking about how Alex was still alive and in protective custody and how nobody must find out.

He had quietly opened the front door to the flat

again and had gone back out, then made more noise when he came in this time. All conversation about Alex had stopped, and Miller hadn't confronted Kim about it.

But he had known. He'd had to keep his mouth shut to keep Harry and Grace safe, but it had eaten away at him, knowing that Harry hadn't really lost his wife, but he, Miller, had. Yes, he had Kim, and he loved her, but losing Carol had taken a lot out of him. And he would have her back in a heartbeat.

FIFTEEN

1983

The boy was a man now. Had been for a long time, and the transition had been an exciting one. Ever since he had killed his sister.

That day, he had gone back home and told his mother that he couldn't find his sister and didn't know where she was. His mother, who was a huge stickler for somebody being on time, went looking for her. She was the one who found her: she walked onto the footbridge and saw her daughter lying on the riverbank below.

A man walking his dog heard her screaming and

rushed over to see what was going on, and he ran along to Broughton Road to use the call box there.

The boy was watching TV when the police came knocking. They told him what had happened and he dug deep then. His cat had died a few months before, and he thought back to the day it had died and started crying, thinking of the animal and not his sister.

It was hectic after that, with his father coming home and telling him that he was to go to his auntie's house while he and his mother went to the mortuary.

His sister wouldn't be coming home.

The boy had been happy after that – happy on the inside, sad on the outside, just to keep up appearances. He had thought he would never see the man again. But he was playing with some friends in St Marks Park one day when he saw the man walking through. He looked over at the boy and smiled, and continued walking towards the pavilion.

The boy excused himself, telling his friends he needed to pee, and he found the man sitting on the steps at one end of the pavilion.

'Did you enjoy it?' the man asked simply.

'Enjoy what?' the boy asked.

He thought the man was going to bandy words

with him, but he came right out with it instead. 'Killing your sister.'

The boy was going to deny everything, and he could have and walked away and nobody would ever have been the wiser. The police thought it was a sad accident, there were no witnesses to say otherwise and no finger of suspicion was ever pointed because there was nothing to be suspicious about.

'Yes,' he said instead.

The man smiled. 'Good. That was just the beginning.'

'What do you mean?' The boy sat on the steps beside his new friend, feeling a rush like he'd never felt before.

'I'm going to teach you how to do it for real. How to get away with it, just like I have.'

At this point, the man could have just been spouting nonsense, living in a fantasy world, or he could have been dangerous to the boy, but the boy sensed that he wasn't in any danger.

'Okay,' he said simply, feeling a sense of empowerment he'd never felt before. His sister had belittled him at every turn, verbally, mentally and physically abusing him at every opportunity. And she'd never been made to pay. Until the day he'd pulled the rope away.

'I have a problem,' the man said. 'I'd like you to help me with it.'

'Okay,' the boy said again.

'Don't worry, I'm not going to let you kill anybody, but you can be there to watch what happens. And then help me dispose of the body.'

The boy nodded, not quite believing what they were going to do. 'When?' he asked simply.

'I'll come and find you closer to the time. Be prepared.'

And the man got up from the steps and walked away.

Three weeks passed before he saw the man next. In the park again.

'This afternoon,' he told the boy.

The boy looked at his watch. 'This is the afternoon.'

'You catch on quickly.'

They walked across St Marks Park, by the strip of allotments, down from the pavilion. Nobody was around except for a dog walker in the distance. If asked, all he would see was a man with a teenager walking away. Nothing remarkable.

They walked down to the railway line and cut along the pathway to Connaught Place. It was thick with overgrown trees where the old railway line had been.

'This stair here,' the man said, pointing to an entrance door.

'I don't understand,' the boy said.

'You will.' Making sure the coast was clear, the man quickly walked across to the stair door and opened it. 'Stay close, say nothing.'

The boy nodded and followed the man along to the first door on the right. There wasn't a name on the door, but the man knew exactly where he was coming to it seemed. He gently rapped on the door.

After perhaps thirty seconds or so, the door was opened by a young woman. She smiled when she saw the man, but then her smile faltered when she saw the boy standing there.

'Who's this?' she said.

'He's my cousin. He's just at a loose end today. Sorry. Can I still come in?'

She smiled again. 'Okay, but you'll have to be quiet. The little one's having a nap.'

'Quiet as a mouse,' the man said. The boy just smiled and nodded, saying nothing.

They went through to the living room and the woman told the boy to have a seat. She had the TV on, but it was at a low volume.

'Would you like something to drink?' she asked the boy.

'No, thank you,' he said.

'Right. Well, play around with the TV, but keep it low,' she said, and smiled at the man again. She looked older than him but not by much and she was pretty.

'We won't be long,' the man said to the boy and they left the living room. He heard voices in another room and they were raised. Not what he had expected when she said to keep quiet.

He got up from the settee and crept through to the lobby.

'This was fun,' he heard the man say, 'but you getting pregnant wasn't part of the deal.'

'It's not like I meant for it to happen.'

There was silence for a bit and the boy scarpered back through to the living room. He heard muted voices this time and then the bedroom door opened.

'We've decided we're going for a walk,' the man said when he came out of the room. Then he turned to the woman. 'Get Helen into her pushchair. Meet us down on the path in five minutes. If you're serious about us being together, I don't want to be here, in *his* house.'

'Okay, relax, sweetheart.' She smiled at the man

and then fussed about getting her sleepy and grumpy daughter into her pushchair. The little girl just looked at the man and the boy before cuddling her teddy and falling back asleep.

They went out into the sunshine, just a group of friends out for a stroll, and they got to a quiet spot on the old railway line, long ago turned into a footpath. They were shaded from the sun by the trees.

'Down here,' the man said, and they walked further down, towards the river.

'He's not due home yet,' the woman said to him, smiling.

'Maybe not, but I wanted to tell you something. This is not going any further. You have to get rid of the baby and stay with your husband.'

The boy's eyes went wide as he looked down at the little girl.

'I didn't mean to get pregnant, but now that I am, I want us to keep it. We can all be together. He knows I'm unhappy. I've threatened to leave him in the past. I'd rather have a life with you.'

The boy felt relief that the little girl wasn't going to come to any harm.

'You're an older woman,' the man said. 'You were okay to have fun with, but I don't want to spend the rest of my life with you.'

At that, the woman's face changed. 'You bastard. You just used me. And now I'm going to have your baby.' Her face was getting red now. 'I'll tell him you raped me.' She turned to the boy. 'You heard me; your cousin raped me.'

The boy couldn't speak, but he watched as the man reached into the overgrown grass at the side of the path and picked up a hammer. Nobody was around here, and they couldn't be seen from anywhere because of the thick, overgrown vegetation.

The woman turned to face the man and he hit her square on the forehead. She mumbled something and fell backwards.

'Come on,' the man said. 'Help me get her over this wall.' Two pairs of work gloves had been hidden alongside the hammer and they put them on after the man tossed the hammer into the bushes.

The boy hadn't realised there was a wall here. It was low and covered in vegetation. He helped the man drag the woman to it and they each lifted an end and hefted her over.

'Go get the girl in case she wakes up.'

The boy brought her into the bushes, but she didn't wake up.

There were allotments on this side.

'This one's not being used,' the man said. 'I picked it for this very purpose. I left the hammer there, brought her down here and now, well, have a look.'

The boy looked behind a hut and saw a shallow grave with an old spade leaning against the hut. The man jumped over the wall. It wasn't a great drop on the other side. The boy jumped down too, adrenaline coursing through him. He felt something inside of him, something alien, a feeling he'd never felt before. He'd thought he would be repulsed at seeing another dead body, but he wasn't. Then he realised she wasn't dead.

'Get her feet,' the man said.

'What?'

'Her feet. Grab them.'

The boy reached down and grabbed the woman by the ankles. Then she was moving, and he thought for a moment that she was struggling, but it was the man who was moving her. He moved forward, his feet splayed, walking like a penguin, until they were at the hole.

No, grave, the boy reminded himself, and then there was sideways motion.

'Swing,' the man said, and they swung her a

couple of times and let her go. She landed in the grave.

More groaning. The boy was pleased to see there was no blood, but there was a massive bruise on her forehead.

'Start shovelling,' the man said.

The boy did as he was told and was sweating by the time he was finished.

An old bench was over to one side and beside it, a homemade cold frame with polythene for glass. It was light and they lifted it over onto the grave. Now it didn't look like freshly dug earth.

'Come on, take those gloves off and let's get the girl back,' the man said. They both took off the gloves and dumped them.

'What are we going to do with her?'

'Put her back inside the house and let her sleep. Her dad will be home later and he'll wonder where his wife went.'

They climbed back over the wall and made their way through the trees to where the little girl was in her pushchair.

She was looking at them. She looked right at the boy and started crying.

'Oh no,' he said, and panic gripped him.

'Hey, where's my girl?' the man said, picking up

the teddy bear that had fallen on the ground. 'Come on, let's go and see Mummy.' He gave the child the stuffed toy and she stopped crying.

'What if somebody sees us?' the boy asked.

'That's part of the thrill. But let's make sure nobody does.'

'What about the hammer?'

'It was an old one that I found in the hut on the allotment,' the man said.

They made it back to the house with no witnesses. They put the little girl in her room and then they left.

Annabelle Hunt was reported missing that evening by her husband when he got home from work. She was never found. Hunt brought his daughter up alone until he had his wife declared dead years later and found somebody else.

SIXTEEN

Present day

'So you see, Helen, that's how your mother died. She was never found, but no doubt when the allotments are sold to a developer, she'll be dug up – just a bag of bones, mind – and that will set off a murder inquiry. But it will lead back to my friend. Who's dead.'

The man thought of the man who had carefully nurtured his desire to kill. Paul Hart.

Of course, it had been a while before he found out Hart's name. There wasn't a need to know; Hart just told him to call him by whatever name he chose.

One day he would be Jimmy, the next Bobby. What-ever name sprang to mind.

He was always *the boy*.

Now he had taken over the mantle of being *the man*. He was the man now that Hart was dead. The baton had been passed to him and he was going to run with it. Hart had taught him many things, but above all: don't get caught. The man had read many stories of how those stupid bastards got caught. Watched TV shows where the murderer was so dumb, it was laughable. Paul Hart had showed him how to do it right.

The early days had been strange to him, his feel-ings all over the place: guilt, sadness, regret, joy. All those feelings coursing through his young body after he killed his sister. But she wasn't his sister exactly. She was his stepsister. He hadn't known that at the time. It wasn't until the day of the funeral approached that he found out. His mother had told him that his own father had died in a train accident. He'd been hit by one. The boy wondered why he had been walking on the train tracks, and it was only years later that he learned that his father was a thug and a thief. He'd just broken into a house and was making off with some jewellery, trying to keep out of sight of the police, when the train came out of the fog and hit him. The jewellery gave him up.

The boy was six months old when his father died, and it was his 'dad' he remembered. The three-year-old girl had always been there, the sister whom his stepdad had brought with him.

It explained a lot, really; she had hated him from the first time she clapped eyes on him. There was no bonding there, no love built up over the years. The boy could never understand why she was so cruel to him, even her own father couldn't understand why she acted up all the time, but at her funeral it all became clear. Deep-seated resentment, the boy's mother said. His sister's resentment towards her 'new' mother had never fully diminished, and she took it out on everybody around her. Fighting at school. Fighting at home, sometimes both physically and verbally.

His mother argued with her husband in the following days, about how his daughter was out of control.

His stepfather didn't want to hear about this but instead found solace in a bottle. The turning point for the boy was when one day the old man was drunk and he looked at the boy and said, 'That should be you lying in the ground.'

That was the end of their relationship right there, and any doubts the boy had had about killing his sister were wiped out in that second.

Paul Hart had taken the boy under his wing after that, showing him the way, teaching him all he knew.

Then Hart had left for London after he met a woman. The boy had felt like killing the woman who was taking his friend away. But he killed a prostitute instead. And showed Hart what he had done.

Hart had clapped him on the shoulder. 'My job here is done,' he said and walked away, smiling.

It would be ten years until they killed together again.

'Your mother was a beautiful woman,' the man said now. He was sitting on a settee and Helen was sitting opposite. They were in the man's house, an old cottage that nobody had been interested in because it was miles from anywhere. The man had bought it with one purpose in mind: to kill.

He didn't live here full time, just at the week-ends sometimes. The nearest neighbour was a mile away and he had only spoken to the old boy once. They'd talked about fishing and hiking, but the old boy had told him that his hiking days were over. Maybe they could go fishing sometime? The man had agreed that would be good but had never taken him. Too many questions would be asked, personal questions like, 'What do you do for a living?' and other nonsense like that. And if the man got too uncomfortable, he'd have to kill the old boy as well.

'Are you married?' Helen asked him.

Christ, now she was starting with the personal questions. The man stared past her at the logs crackling in the fire. He'd never been able to hold down a proper relationship. They all started asking personal questions of course, that was to be assumed, and he'd had to lie to each and every one of them. He didn't want them to get to know the real him. How could he? He couldn't let them get inside his head. He had used them for a while, making out he was the perfect boyfriend. Caring, loving, protective. His fictitious mother and father were long dead, he had no siblings. He was on his own. Which mirrored his real life but without all the added drama.

'Why do you want to know if I'm married?' the man asked.

'I'm bored. I just thought we could have a little conversation. Plus, I need to pee.'

'Again?' he said, looking her in the eyes this time.

'You don't just pee once a day, do you?'

'Well...no, of course not.'

'Well then, I need to pee again.'

He tilted his head back and let out a sigh in an exasperated way before standing up. 'I'm going to unlock the handcuffs and then escort you to the bathroom. Don't do anything stupid, or make me do anything I'll regret.'

'I won't.'

He unlocked the handcuffs and stood back, ready to punch her, but she just stretched and groaned as her muscles relaxed. He grabbed her by the elbow and escorted her along the hallway to where the small bathroom was. The guest bathroom and she was a guest here.

He let her go inside and listened at the door, making sure she was indeed peeing. It wasn't something he liked doing, but he did it out of necessity.

Then he walked away, out the front door, and stopped to take in the view of the sun setting below the hills in the distance. There was no sign of anybody else because no traffic passed by here.

He walked round the side of the house to where his old Subaru was parked. He saw Helen sitting behind the wheel, the driver's door wide open. He took the car keys out of his pocket and tossed them into the air and then realised they made no noise. So he whistled and watched her turn to look at him.

'Shall I get the kettle on? Have a nice cuppa?'

Helen got out of the car and gently closed the door. 'Why not? It doesn't look like I'm going anywhere.'

SEVENTEEN

Max Hold got out of the car at South Queensferry, back where Alex had picked him up at Port Edgar Marina.

'See you here in the morning?' he said to her, ducking his head back into the car.

'I'll wait in the café again.'

'Cheers.'

He shut the door and she drove away, heading up to the A90. It felt strange, going home to a place that had never been her home. It was Harry's home, and would have been Morgan Allan's home too if she'd played her cards right. Or had been in the relation-ship for the right reasons. But now she was dead and Alex was replacing her.

Conflicting thoughts jumped through her brain.

She herself had been dead in the eyes of her husband and for all intents and purposes, the world. Was Morgan Allan really dead? They had faked Alex's death saying that she'd had a ruptured brain aneurysm, but Morgan had been shot in the heart and the head. Unless some special effects were used, Alex was pretty sure Morgan was gone from Harry's life.

Now this was going to be *Alex's* home, but for the life of her she couldn't think of Murrayfield as anywhere but Harry's home.

She was starting to get a headache, so she switched on the radio and listened to some meaningless tunes. If she was honest with herself, part of her missed going back to the house by the loch. She had missed Grace of course, but she had almost got used to the living situation. Except for the part where she had recently run away and gone back to the flat in Comely Bank. Anger had driven her, but not anger against Harry; anger at whoever had been doing this, making her live away from home.

She was into Edinburgh now and had to think about how to get home without resorting to her phone's navigation app. After a wrong turn or two, she made it back.

She felt like a stranger going into the house, but

Harry came out of the living room to greet her, carrying their daughter, and all doubts were swept away.

'Hi, honey,' Harry said. Then to Grace: 'Here's Mummy.' Their daughter smiled and put her hands out for Alex.

'Hi, honey,' Alex said, and took her daughter, giving her a big hug. Then she puckered her lips for Harry. She noticed his slight hesitation but kept her position, and he stepped forward and gently kissed her.

'How was your day?' he asked her. She told him briefly about the postmortem and the hike up the hill.

'Hi!' Jessica said, coming out of the kitchen into the large hallway.

'Hi, sis.' The words felt strange coming out, but Alex managed to smile. She handed the toddler back to Harry. 'I need to use the bathroom. It's been a long drive.'

She could feel the two of them watching her as she went upstairs. She locked herself in the bathroom and had a good cry.

EIGHTEEN

Calvin Stewart looked for a parking space outside his flat, going round the block twice. 'Fucking electric car chargers taking up normal spaces,' he muttered to himself, then saw a car pull out round the other side of the bowling club. He squeezed his car in and got out, shaking his head. He hadn't realised that Edinburgh had gone mad. Electric car chargers, cycle lanes everywhere. The clown who was running this show had no fucking clue what he was doing when it came to transport. He certainly had a future in being a janny.

Up in the flat, DSup Lynn McKenzie was waiting for him.

'I went along to Waitrose and got some beers,' she said. 'I'll put something in the oven.'

'As long as it's not your heid.'

She laughed. 'I'm not at that stage of our relationship yet.'

He kissed her. 'What am I going to do when you move back to Glasgow?'

'I'm sure you'll manage.'

'What do you say I take you out to dinner instead?'

'I'm open to suggestions.'

'How about the Scran and Scallie round the corner? Harry said it's magic.'

'Let me get my jacket.'

They walked round to the main road, where the restaurant was. It spanned two store fronts divided by an outside stairway. They went in and were shown to a table at the front, overlooking the road.

The waiter took their orders and came back with their starters of haggis, neeps and tatties.

'Jesus, this is delish,' Stewart said as he tucked into the haggis ball.

Lynn agreed that it was.

'Paul Hart's not finished, is he?' she said as they waited on their main courses.

'No. I think he knew he was dying, that the last heart attack was just around the corner, so he was making his final plans.'

'Sounds like he was working with somebody all along. I mean, it's not as if he could just recruit somebody and say, "Hey, you fancy helping me to kill people?"'

'It would seem that way. But how long has it been going on? His associate must be very clever if nobody knows he exists.'

'That's why it makes sense that they've been working together for a long time. They've honed their skills, and Hart knew when he was gone, his other half would be more than capable of carrying on without him.'

The waiter appeared with steak pie for Stewart and ham hock for Lynn. They were more like works of art than meals.

'This is a fabulous meal,' Lynn said. 'There's wine in the fridge too, upstairs.'

'We should tan it.'

'I can't argue with that,' Lynn said.

'But seriously, we're going to get teams out to Paul Hart's previous addresses. He lived here in Edinburgh, outside of Glasgow in Wishaw, and down in London. That we know of.'

'It's scary to think that there's somebody else out there with Hart's agenda.'

'It is. We need to tear Paul Hart's life apart.'

They finished their meal, and headed back to the flat.

NINETEEN

The café at the Port Edgar Marina was becoming a second office, Alex thought as Neil McGovern sat himself down with two coffees.

'I couldn't remember if he took sugar or not,' McGovern said, 'so I didn't buy him one.'

'Probably best to err on the side of caution,' Alex said. 'He can always add the sugar, but he can't take it out.'

'How very true.' He took a sip of his coffee and leaned back in the chair. 'How are you doing?' he asked Alex.

'One day at a time. I spoke to my stepson, Chance, last night. He was totally shocked, but Harry had spoken to him first. We both cried on the phone. But to be honest, I don't know who's more surprised by all of this, me or Harry, and I already knew I wasn't dead. We'll get there. I'm determined to make it work, Neil. I've clung on to that for the best part of a year. I won't let go now.'

'Good. I'm glad to hear that. Just remember, you'll both need counselling, but it's your choice if you actually want to go or not. We have a great team who work with people who are going into witness protection. Or else you can go out for a drink on the town with Kim. She's always available.'

'I know. I appreciate that.' Alex drank some of her coffee. 'Look, what I did, running away to Edinburgh, dodging the people who were looking after me, well, it was my fault, not theirs. I wouldn't want Simon and Steffi to get into trouble over what I did.'

'They won't. They're both great agents. Maybe a little retraining and that will be that. Trust me, I don't want to lose them.'

Just then, Max Hold walked in, looking fresher than he had the day before.

'Grab yourself a coffee, son. I wasn't sure how you took it.'

'I'm fine, boss,' Max said, sitting down opposite McGovern. 'Morning, Alex.'

'Morning, sir.'

'The plumbers were in yesterday fitting the

washing machine and doing a few bits and bobs,' McGovern said. 'The decorators will be in today in force, and you'll be able to move your furniture in after tomorrow.'

Max looked at him. 'What you saw was it. One chair, one bed, an old TV and some cooking utensils and pots and pans.'

'Christ, talk about minimalist,' McGovern said.

'I had more stuff, but it didn't make it any further than the M25. It was an old removals truck and it broke down and caught fire, taking the rest of my stuff with it.'

'A chance to do some shopping,' Alex said. 'Lucky duck.'

'I hate shopping at the best of times, so I'm going to wing it. IKEA will be my best friend.'

'At least your house will be habitable now,' McGovern said. 'Quite a nice wee place you've got there, son. I'm envious.'

'You live in Trinity, Neil. I hardly think my place in Anstruther competes with that.'

'I would love a nice wee seaside place. Take the bairns over to play on the beach. But the wife likes Spain now that she's retired.'

'I don't blame her,' Alex said. 'It's like Portobello without getting your wig blown off.'

'It's called fresh air, Alex. It didn't do Kim any harm when she was growing up.'

'Each to their own,' Max said.

'Right then, how did your little trip go yesterday?' McGovern asked.

Max filled him in.

'Alex's husband called me this morning,' McGovern said. 'Told me about a missing woman called Helen Marsh. I want you to go and speak to her husband, who reported her missing. It might not be connected to our case, but get some background on him and his wife.'

'Has she gone missing before?' Max asked.

'That's what you're going to find out today, son. You're going to do a complete background on her. I want the works. Call me at the end of the day and I'll have a little chinwag with Harry.'

'Will do.' Max nodded to Alex. 'You still okay with driving?'

'I am. But we can take your car if you want.'

McGovern made a tutting sound. 'If you saw what his scrapper looked like, you would want to take an Uber. Trust me, take your own car.'

'It's a manky pool car,' Alex said.

'It has brakes and a steering wheel, doesn't it? Then it's a whole lot better than Max's car.'

Max smiled at her. 'It's a classic Morgan. I'm just getting her made roadworthy.'

'He thinks he's Inspector Morse, driving about in an old classic car.' McGovern laughed and stood up. 'You need modern technology in your life, son.'

'They're an investment,' Max replied.

'So is a hip replacement.' McGovern patted him on the shoulder. 'I look forward to hearing what our Mr Marsh has to say.'

McGovern walked out of the café and Alex lifted her disposable coffee cup. 'Shall we hit the road? Neil already gave me the address. It's in Dalgety Bay.'

They walked out into the sunshine and across to Alex's car.

'Where do you keep the Morgan?' she asked.

'There's a classic car place in Kirkcaldy that's doing it up. It should be ready in a month or so.'

'Sounds good.'

Over the Queensferry Crossing, Alex cut off through Inverkeithing.

'You know this place well?' Max asked her.

'Harry's mum lived through here. His brother still does, but his mum passed.' She looked at him. 'Didn't you look me up?'

He drank some of the coffee and looked sideways at her. 'What do you mean?'

'Didn't you look at my obituary? The one Neil had made up.'

'No, I didn't do anything like that. You're a colleague who's on temporary assignment with me and that's it.'

They didn't say much more as she drove, taking a right at the first roundabout leading into Dalgety Bay and following the instructions from her phone until they stopped outside a detached, two-storey brick house.

'Nice place,' Max said.

They walked up to the front door and their knock was answered by a man who looked like he was in his early forties, clean shaven with short hair. They identified themselves.

'Have you found her?' Roger Marsh asked.

'No, but we'd like to come in and have a chat about her,' Alex said.

'Okay. Yes, of course,' he said, stepping aside to let them in. He closed the door and led them past a staircase and through to the living room.

It was immaculate, with a white leather couch facing the gas fire and another chair near sliding glass doors that led to a back garden. A TV sat in one corner, switched off.

'Please, sit down,' Max said to Marsh.

'Yes, yes, okay,' he replied, sitting on the chair. Max and Alex sat on the couch.

'Do you have any family, Mr Marsh?' Max asked. 'Children?'

'No. Helen doesn't want any.'

'Any family close by? In case we need to call somebody for support.'

'Just my father, up in Kirkcaldy. But I'm a doctor, I can take bad news. Like when my mother died. She got hit by a car. I deal with death all the time.'

'What kind of doctor are you, if you don't mind me asking?' Alex said.

'Accident and Emergency. I work in the Royal Infirmary in Edinburgh.'

'Has your wife done anything like this before? Disappeared, maybe come back after a period of time?' Max asked.

Marsh shook his head. 'Nothing like this, ever. But it's like bloody history repeating itself.'

Both detectives perked up at this.

'What do you mean?' Max asked.

Marsh looked at them in turn. 'Her mother disappeared too, when Helen was three. Annabelle.

She was never found. Nobody knew if it was foul play or what, but her mother left Helen in the house on her own, and when her father came home, there was no sign of her mother. They searched for her. It was in the papers, on the news. They searched for months, but they found nothing. And now Helen has gone missing. I can't believe it.'

'Do you know if her mother could have run off with somebody?' Alex asked.

'They looked into that, but her father said no, they were happy. Then the old bastard admitted months before he died that her mother did indeed have a boyfriend. He didn't tell the police at the time because he thought it would bring shame on him. Or make him a suspect. There was a possibility that Annabelle had left with her other man, but why wouldn't she have taken Helen?'

'And nothing was ever heard from her again?'

'No.'

'Do you think Helen could have gone looking for her mother, if she thought she might be alive?' Max asked.

'I don't think so. I mean, unless her mother had been in contact, where would she start looking?'

'There haven't been any strange phone calls

recently?' Alex asked. 'No hang-ups, or strange men asking to talk to Helen?'

'What are you saying? That she was messing about on me?' Marsh said. 'No, that's not possible. You wouldn't think that if you knew Helen like I know her.'

'Does Helen work?' Alex asked.

'Yes. She's a nurse.'

Alex noticed he said *is* and not *was*. This had tripped up suspects in the past. 'Where was she a nurse?'

'At the Royal in Edinburgh. We used to live through there, but the house prices were so much better here. Now I wish we'd never moved.'

Alex looked at the man and had a thought: *I don't think it would have mattered.*

'One more question, Mr Marsh,' Alex said. 'What was Helen's maiden name?'

'Hunt. She was Helen Hunt when I met her.'

TWENTY

Harry was in the kitchen finishing his breakfast when Jessica came in, with Grace all ready to go to the nursery.

'Alex is away,' he said.

'I know. She came in to see Grace. She's away to Fife again.'

Harry stood up from the table and put his plate and mug in the dishwasher. 'This will help her get back into the swing of things again,' he said. 'Get back into the swing of police work.'

'It must have been so hard being away for so long,' Jessica said. 'And doing nothing with her day when she was used to being out and about. I know it would drive me mental.'

'It's going to be a tough adjustment for all of us.'

'Neil McGovern is working closely with her, and Max Hold will be with her, so she'll be fine.'

They said their goodbyes and Harry left the house, looking both ways up the street. He was ninety per cent sure he was safe, but in his line of work, being a hundred per cent could cost you your life.

He was about to get into his car when his phone rang.

'Hello?'

'Skellett here, sir. We got a shout. Body of a woman found on the Roseburn path in Russell Road.'

'Is the team there?'

'Some of us are here.'

'I'll be there in five.'

He got into his Jag and made his way to the main road. The traffic was backing up going into Edin-burgh from the west side of the city, so he put his blues and twos on, making his way past the heavy traffic.

Round into Russell Road near the tram bridge. Police vehicles were there and the mortuary van was in attendance. An ambulance crew too, but they were waiting for the stand-down.

Lillian O'Shea was there, along with Skellett and

Elvis. Then Harry saw Frank Miller coming out of the forensics tent.

'Morning, boss,' they said to Harry.

'Morning. What have we got?' The sun was out and the day was warm and dry. He could already feel himself sweating.

'Female, aged thirty-five, lives in South Gyle,' Miller said. 'It's a victim like Hart's.'

'How do you know?'

'The heart drawn in lipstick on her chest, above her breast near the collarbone.'

'What's her name?'

'Marion Todd.'

'I wonder what she was doing along here?' Harry said, looking around at the flats next to the footpath.

'You should talk to the doc. She's in the tent,' Miller said.

Harry walked to the start of the path alongside Miller.

'This goes up to the old railway line, and there's another path that leads down to Balbirnie Place on the other side,' Miller said.

'There are uniforms doing a door-to-door, I assume?' Harry said.

'Elvis and Lillian are dealing with that.'

Harry shook his head. 'Soon there won't be enough space left to build flats on.'

'Oh, I'm sure they'll find somewhere, Harry. There's always the castle. They can turn the barracks into some flats.'

Gus Weaver and Sticks, the mortuary assistants, were waiting outside the tent. Sticks looked pale, like she was sick.

'You okay, Sticks?' Harry asked.

'I just feel a bit off today.'

Harry hadn't seen her this bad at a crime scene before and knew it wasn't the sight of a dead body that was causing it.

'Tell your boss you feel sick if you have to go home,' he said.

'I will.' She nodded and held on to Weaver.

'You want to sit down?' Weaver said, concern spreading across his face.

'Sorry, Gus, I don't feel well at all. Just give me a minute, I'm sure I'll be fine.'

Weaver held on to her for support.

'Look after yourself,' Harry said.

'Forensics have photographed and videoed the victim,' Miller said as they entered the tent. Finbar O'Toole was inside.

'Morning, Harry,' he said.

'Morning.'

Harry walked over to where the victim lay, on the grass on the side of the path, the side wall of the tent behind her. He saw a woman who was overweight but not unattractive. She had dyed blonde hair and was wearing make-up and clothes that suggested she had been on a night out. The lifeless skin colour told him she had been dead for hours.

Her blouse had been ripped open, but her breasts hadn't been exposed, the black bra still in place. A small red heart had been drawn on her chest, near her collarbone. Harry realised that the black bra had concealed a stab mark. Her skirt was down to her knees.

'Has she been sexually assaulted?' Harry asked.

Finbar shook his head. 'No. I had a look, but there's no evidence down there that I can see. I'll be able to tell for sure when I have her on the table. It looks like the only wound is the stab to her heart and it would have been fatal, looking at the position of it. The heart would have stopped very soon after that, so there hasn't been much bleeding.'

'No sign of a weapon?' Harry looked at Miller.

'They've been searching, and they'll do it again once the victim's been moved and the tent taken away. But nothing so far.'

'The wound is small and circular. Like the weapon was an ice pick or maybe an awl. Something like that,' Finbar said.

'Time of death?'

Finbar looked at Harry. 'I'd say between eleven last night and one this morning. Eight to ten hours ago.'

'Thanks, Fin.'

'No problem, Harry.'

Harry and Miller left the tent.

'I thought we'd seen the last of the killings when Hart was put away for the rest of his life,' Gus Weaver said.

'So did we, Gus,' Harry said.

'It's so scary for women,' Sticks added in her Polish accent. She was sitting down on the pathway, her knees drawn up.

'Everybody has to be extra vigilant,' Weaver added. 'When you're out playing in your band, don't travel alone; share a ride or take a taxi home.'

'He's right,' Skellett said, coming up to them. 'Young lassies should be carrying fucking pepper spray. Or a knife.'

'We have enough stabbings in this city,' Harry said.

'Cut his baws off then, boss. Either way, you do

what you have to do to get away if somebody comes near you, hen.' Skellett nodded to Sticks.

'Listen to him, Sticks,' Weaver said. 'There's a nutter running about.'

But Sticks wasn't listening; she had her head between her knees and was trying not to be sick.

'After you two get back to the mortuary, you should go home,' Harry said.

Sticks made a grunting noise, then keeled over.

Harry shouted for the ambulance crew and they came running over, one of them with a bag he had grabbed from the ambulance when he saw Sticks fall sideways.

They attended to her. The ambulance man with the bag, a young guy called Martin whom Harry recognised from other scenes, turned to his partner and told her to get the gurney.

'Is she going to be okay?' Harry asked the young man.

'Looks like she's just fainted, but we'll take her to the Royal just to be on the safe side.'

They got her onto the gurney with the help of some uniforms, and she was put into the ambulance and whisked away.

'Jesus, I hope she's alright,' Weaver said. 'I've never seen her like that before.'

'They'll take good care of her, Gus,' Miller said.

'Right,' Harry said, 'Elvis and Lillian are running the show regarding the door-to-door...' Just then another car pulled up.

'Calvin,' Harry said unnecessarily.

Stewart got out of his car and walked up to the crime-scene tape.

'You can't come in here,' a uniform said.

'Harry! Get this fucking bawbag to get out of my way before I rattle his fucking jaw.'

'What did you say, cheeky bast–' the uniform started to say, but Harry put up a hand.

'This is Detective Superintendent Stewart. He's head of our MIT now.'

'Sorry, sir, I didn't recognise you,' the uniform said, lifting the tape.

'You will from now on, though, eh?' Stewart replied, ducking under. 'I got a call from control about this lassie,' he said to Miller and Harry.

'It's the same MO as Hart's,' Miller said. 'The heart drawn on her chest.'

'But now he's passed the baton to somebody else and this fucker is running with it,' Stewart said.

'It would seem that way,' Harry said. Then his phone rang. It was Alex. His heart missed a beat as he answered. 'Hello?'

'*Harry, it's Alex.*'

'Is everything okay?'

'*It is. I just wanted to check in. We spoke to Roger Marsh, husband of Helen Marsh, the woman who's missing. I think she was taken by Hart's accomplice. Her maiden name is Hunt. She was Helen Hunt. The name you told me Hart's cellmate gave to you.*'

'Hart told Hughes that he had killed Helen Hunt.'

'*This is a different one, but I think he was playing games. Helen's mother went missing back in 1980, when Helen was only three. Her name was Annabelle though. Her daughter is Helen. Hart would have known this. It seems a strange coincidence. What if Hart killed Helen's mother all those years ago and he mentioned Helen to his cell mate? And he intended for his partner in crime to abduct Helen?*'

'Has there been any communication from Helen's abductor?'

'*No, nothing. I don't think we're going to find her alive.*'

'You're right. But if he's killed her, then he might dump her soon or wait until he thinks the timing is right. We found a victim this morning, so he'll want that to be our main focus.'

'*Sounds about right.*'

'We'll head back to the station just now and find a next of kin for this woman, then go talk to somebody.'

'We're going to look at where Amy Dunn lived. Talk to some of her friends. I'll see you tonight for dinner?'

'Okay. But listen, would you be up to you and me going out for a meal?'

'Of course I would. I'd like that.'

'Great. I'll let Jessica know, and she'll be only too happy to babysit, I'm sure.'

'I can't wait.' There was a pause. *'I love you, Harry. I always will.'*

'I love you too,' he said with no hesitation.

He hung up and thought for a second he had been talking to a ghost. That was something he would have to get over.

TWENTY-ONE

It was a nice day for a drive along the Fife coastal road if they had been going out for a picnic, or even just a wander along the promenade, with a clear view from Kirkcaldy all the way across the forth to Edinburgh, but Alex and Max were here on business.

Alex turned into the small car park of the large building on the main street and followed it round to the back.

'This is the old canvas works building, Neil told me,' Max said. 'It housed Fife College too before they left years ago.'

'And like Edinburgh, it was turned into housing,' Alex said, parking up.

They walked to the door and up to Amy Dunn's flat.

'Neil gave me the key,' Max said. He opened the front door cautiously, and they entered.

There was a bathroom on the left, empty. Alex walked ahead and saw the bedroom with the bed that hadn't been slept in for days. She joined Max in the combined living room and kitchen. It was tidy, with a couple of magazines left on the coffee table. The kitchen area was behind the couch and wooden stairs led up to a mezzanine area with a dining table.

'Nice place,' Alex said.

'It belongs to Neil's office. Amy was renting it, if anybody asked, and the bills were in her name for the sake of appearances,' Max replied.

There were letters on the kitchen counter, opened and put into two piles. One looked like junk mail, while the other looked like bills and things to be taken care of.

It made Alex sad to think that Amy would never be coming back again to deal with them.

There was nothing in the flat that stuck out. No sign of any man staying there.

'Maybe Amy had casual sex with a man and got caught out,' Max said.

'Or she hid her boyfriend well. I wonder if she told Neil about him?' Alex said.

'Come on, let's go and check out where she worked.'

They left the flat and returned to the car and drove the short distance to the Kirkcaldy Galleries, a combined museum and public library.

They went in and turned into the Café Wemyss, where Amy had worked, and approached the counter. It was warm and didn't smell like a museum typically does.

'Can I help you?' said the woman behind the counter. She was old and shuffled about like she could do with a Zimmer.

'I'm here about Amy Dunn,' Max replied, and they showed their warrant cards.

'You want a bun? What kind?'

'No, no, Amy Dunn,' Alex said, raising her voice but at the same time trying to keep it low. Like an exaggerated whisper.

'Have I done what?' The woman looked alarmed.

'No. The girl who worked here beside you. Amy.'

Another woman stepped behind the counter. 'Sorry, Agnes is a volunteer. She's hard of hearing.'

'We're here about Amy Dunn,' Max said, starting again.

'Yes, she works here. But not today. She was supposed to be working, but she didn't turn up. I'm helping out instead.'

'We'd like to talk to you about her,' Max said. He and Alex walked to one side and watched as the woman followed, on her side of the counter.

'Is anything wrong?'

Max looked round before answering. 'I'm sorry to tell you that Amy is deceased.'

The woman gasped and clutched her chest for a moment, as if checking to see that her pearls were still there. 'Dead? What happened?'

'It's still an ongoing investigation, and I need to ask you some questions.'

'Oh yes, yes, anything I can help you with.'

'Did Amy seem troubled by anything recently?'

'Or anyone?' Alex added.

'Nobody that I know of,' said the lady. 'We do get weirdos in here at times, but that's only occasionally. She was very happy. The happiest I've seen her in a long time. Probably because of her new boyfriend.'

'Can you tell us more about this boyfriend?' Max asked.

'She'd met him here, in the café. He just started

talking to her one day, said he was interested in art and came here on the train.'

'The train station is right next door, isn't it?' Alex said.

'Yes, you just walk across the car park and you're right in the station. So he would come through here and they would chat, and one day he asked her out and she said yes.'

'Did they meet here all the time?' Alex asked.

'Oh aye, all the time. Sometimes she would be working so it was easier for him to come here. She worked part time in the Royal in Edinburgh too, but she was here a lot.'

'Do you know the boyfriend's name?'

'Oh, now I do. What is it again?' The woman put her hand on her chin and stared down at the counter.

An old man appeared for another Americano and Alex waved her warrant card at him and gently told him to come back. The old boy whispered a quick 'fuck's sake' under his breath and was going to add more but thought it was better not to spend the night in Kirkcaldy holding cells, which were just round the corner.

Alex and Max stood patiently, Max wondering if it would be against protocol to ask for his own Americano since he was here, but he eyed up the scones instead.

'Marsh,' the woman said, dispelling any thoughts of a scone and jam.

'Do you remember the first name?' Alex asked. *Please God.*

'Hmm. What was it again? I only met him once. I didn't like him.' The woman leaned in for the last part, the ringleader in a gossip club. 'Roger!' she said, leaning back. 'His name was Roger Marsh.'

TWENTY-TWO

'Listen, Harry, son, you wait until they finish up here and I'll take Charlie-boy along to see if we can find a next of kin. I'll have the boy drive us.' Stewart looked around. 'Elvis! Get your fucking arse over here.'

Elvis walked over. 'How can I help, sir?'

'You can drive my car. We're going to South Gyle. Charlie! With me.'

Skellett came walking over, leaning on his walking stick. 'Going for a coffee, are we?'

'Coffee? Lazy bastard. When you've done some work, maybe you'll get a coffee. And you're paying.'

'What? The lad's coming. He'll be more than happy to pay. Eh, Elvis?'

'I forgot my wallet, sir,' Elvis replied with a deadpan face.

'See? Forgot his wallet,' Stewart said. 'You could let that smelly fucking thing you call a wallet see the light of day now and again. Let the moths get a breath of fresh air.'

'When are you going back to Glasgow?' Skellett asked as he got into the back seat of the car.

'Cheeky bastard. By the time I'm finished with you, you'll wish I was going back to Glasgow.'

'I already wish that now,' Skellett said, slamming the back door.

'Christ, is that fucking door shut properly? Ham-fisted fanny. And you, Heid-the-Baw,' he shouted over to the uniform as Elvis got in behind the wheel. 'Get the fucking tape out of our way.'

The uniform looked like he wished he'd joined the army instead of the police but lifted the tape for the car to move under.

'In his head, he just stuck the vickies up at me,' Stewart said.

Skellett started yanking the seat belt back and forth.

'Easy! Fuck. You trying to rip the bastard out or something? This is my own car, not some polis shite.'

'Fucking belt's stuck,' Skellett complained, yanking it harder.

'How, Charlie, how? What do you do to these

belts to get them stuck? I know you're a fat bastard but not that big the belt won't go round you.'

'Fuck it,' Skellett said, letting the belt go. 'If we crash and I get thrown out, then so be it. But answer my question: when are you going back through?'

'Why do you want to know?'

'I want to go with you. We could get a few beers, reminisce about the good times we had back then.'

'That's right,' said Stewart, 'make Elvis think we were a couple. I don't recall ever socialising with you.'

'He's a liar, Elvis. We would go out on the lash all the time.'

Elvis concentrated on the driving.

'We were colleagues, Charlie,' Stewart reminded him.

Skellett laughed, then Elvis made a sharp right turn and Skellett fell sideways on the back seat.

'See? That's what he was like when he had a drink in him. And now he's sober. I think.'

'I never drink and work, Calvin, you know that.'

'You've got no fucking filter, have you? Now, sit up and give it a rest.'

Skellett chuckled and straightened himself up.

They finally reached South Gyle.

'Gogarloch Hog,' Skellett said, reading the street sign.

'Even though it's spelled H-A-U-G-H, it's pronounced "Hawk", like the bird,' Elvis said.

'And they pay some daft bastard in the council to make up shite like this? Whatever he's getting paid, he needs to learn to read and write, instead of just coming out with any old pish. Hawk indeed,' Skellett said.

Elvis parked outside a detached house with a small Nissan in the driveway. All the curtains were closed.

Stewart was first out the car, then Elvis, and they waited while Skellett banged his walking stick about.

'Christ, just stand there and watch me struggle,' he said when he got the door open.

'Okay then,' Stewart said, leaving Skellett to get out of the car while he marched up to the door and banged on it. Elvis grabbed Skellett's arm and hauled him out.

'Easy, ya hoor. You're rougher than that gawk.'

'Who's a fucking gawk?' Stewart said, turning round to him.

'You,' Skellett said. 'Time was, you would help in the back of the van when we were on surveillance. You would help me get into my costume when we –'

Stewart held up a hand. 'Stop fucking talking. You and your vans. Why don't you sell that jalopy you have and buy yourself an old BT van? Park outside old women's houses and pretend you're from the gas board.'

Skellett shook his head as Stewart banged on the door again. 'Slavering pish. BT van and pretend I'm from the gas board. Who would fall for that?'

'Not me,' Elvis said.

'Don't fucking encourage him,' Stewart said. 'When he retires, he'll be on the TV: have you seen this man, driving an old Transit van?'

Stewart turned when the front door was thrown open.

'If you're selling fucking religion, you can piss off!' the man said.

'Keep your boxers on there, son. Polis.' Stewart flashed his warrant card.

'What do you want? I'm on the night shift.'

'We want Michael Todd.'

'That's me,' the man said.

'We want to come in and talk to you.'

'Is it important?' The man screwed his face up.

'There's three detectives at your door. Do you think we're selling double-glazing? Of course it's important. Now, we can discuss your business on your doorstep, or you can invite us inside. I don't give a toss either way. But I don't talk in a low voice, just so you know.'

The man tutted and stepped aside, and they trooped in, Skellett watching where he was placing his walking stick.

'Living room's on the right,' Todd said.

They went in and stood around, waiting for Todd to join them. He came in, scratching a place round the back where they couldn't see. His hair was cut short and he had stubble. He was muscular but short. Still, Stewart sized him up and knew the man could probably fight.

'If you see one, sit on it,' Todd said. He plonked himself down in a chair, putting a cushion in his lap.

Stewart and Elvis sat down, while Skellett elected to stand and lean on his walking stick.

'Right, you have five minutes, then I'm off back to my scratcher.'

'Your wife's deid,' Skellett said, pain shooting through his knee.

'What?' Todd sat forward in his chair. 'What do you mean, she's deid?'

'She was found this morning,' Stewart said. 'So we need to know where you were last night.'

'I was at work. All night!' Todd's voice bordered on panic.

'What is it you do?' Stewart asked, although he knew the answer. He'd already checked the name against the house number.

'I'm a prison officer.'

'Did you go out anywhere before your shift?'

'No. I slept until late afternoon. Marion came home, we had dinner and then she got ready to go out. She and her pals were having a girls' night out at somebody's house.'

'Did you notice she wasn't home when you got in from work?' Elvis asked.

'No. I was working until late, filling in reports. Marion leaves for work around eight, so it wouldn't be unusual for her to be gone when I got in. I didn't think anything of it until you lot came knocking.' Todd shook his head and put his face in his hands for a few seconds. 'How did she die? Was she hit by a car or something?'

'No, she was murdered,' Stewart said, looking at Skellett, silently asking if he wanted to jump in. Skellett was busy staring at Todd.

'Murdered? How? In her pal's flat?'

'No,' Skellett answered. 'Do you know what friend she was seeing last night?'

'Christ knows. There's a bunch of them. They go to each other's houses, including here. They take it in turns.'

'You mean to say that your wife went out and she didn't tell you where she was going?' Stewart said.

'She probably mentioned the name of the friend, but I don't know where they all live. If there was an emergency, I'd just call her.'

'Could I look at your mobile phone?' Stewart asked.

'Aye, of course. I'll go and get it. It's in my bedroom.' Todd got up and left the room.

'Get a patrol car to come to this address,' Stewart told Elvis.

'Yes, sir.' Elvis left the room and stepped outside the house.

'I thought you were going to blurt out where she was murdered,' Stewart said to Skellett.

'This is not my first rodeo, Calvin. I'm not just going to blurt something out. Like you blurted out that time when you were pished that you were a copper, just before that lassie –'

Todd thumped down the stairs and came back in. Stewart reached out and took Todd's iPhone, which he had unlocked.

'Help yourself. Look at anything you want. I sent

a text to Marion after she told me she had got to her friend's house safely. She always texted, no matter where she was going.' Todd sat back down and stared off into space for a few seconds. 'Where was she murdered?' he asked.

Stewart took his eyes off the phone for a moment, deciding now that there was no harm in telling Todd; the news would be broadcasting it soon anyway, when the vultures got wind of it.

'Roseburn. Russell Road to be exact. Which one of her friends lives there?'

'Christ, I don't know. There's a whole gang of them. I only know some of their names, not all of them. It's people she works with.'

'Where does she work?'

'She's a nurse at the Royal Infirmary.'

'When was the last time you spoke to her?' Skellett asked.

'I told you, she sent me a text.'

'I meant actually talked to her?'

Todd thought about it for a moment. 'Last night before she went out. Then she sent me the text.'

'Do you know if anybody had any beef with your wife?' Stewart asked.

'If they did, she didn't tell me.'

'No problems at work?' Skellett asked.

'Not that I know of. As far as I know, everything was fine.' Todd rubbed his eyes.

'Was your wife having an affair?' Skellett asked.

'What? Of course not,' Todd replied, indignation thick in his voice.

'It happens. Sometimes the husband finds out, decides to punish the wife.'

'I told you, I was at work. Call the prison; they'll confirm that.'

'Do you need us to call anybody, Mr Todd?' Stewart asked.

Todd shook his head just as Elvis came back in and nodded to the boss.

'We'll need you to come down to the mortuary and make a formal identification, and then come to Fettes Station to make a statement.'

'When?'

'Now. There's patrol officers on their way to take you to the mortuary and then Fettes. You'll need to get dressed.'

Todd nodded.

'One more thing before we go,' Skellett said. 'Did you ever interact with Paul Hart before he died?'

'Yes,' said Todd. 'I worked on his wing. I was one of the accompanying officers who escorted him to the hospital. Why?'

'Did you ever get in a conversation with him?' Stewart asked.

'He was the one who always spoke first. I mean, when we weren't giving him instructions. He tried to make conversation, but none of us were having it. We're not paid to have social hour with inmates but to be professional at all times.'

'Did Hart ever talk about his victims?'

'That's all he ever talked about, how he had killed dozens of women. But they all say that. Every one of them wants to be the hard man so they don't get picked on.'

'What was he like when he was taken to the hospital?' Skellett asked.

'He was in pain after the heart attack. But good old Hart, he kept on boasting how he had killed a ton of women.'

Stewart looked at Todd. He didn't want to tell him about the heart drawn on his wife's chest.

'Did you see him interacting with anybody else while he was in the hospital?' Stewart asked.

'Just hospital staff. No member of the public got near him. Only staff.'

'You're sure? None of your mates could have slipped up and let somebody in?'

'No, not at all. We made sure it was only people

who wore badges in the hospital. Doctors, nurses, technicians. No public.'

Stewart nodded, then stood up. 'The patrol will take you to the station now, Mr Todd. We have to rule you out as a suspect.'

Todd nodded. 'I'll go and get dressed.'

Outside, a patrol car pulled up and Stewart waved to the uniforms to get in the house and he briefed them both.

'You think Hart's accomplice did this?' he asked Skellett and Elvis.

'Who else?' Skellett answered. 'Especially since she has the heart drawn on her.'

'Let's keep an open mind,' Stewart answered as they went back to the car.

TWENTY-THREE

It was clouding over by the time Alex and Max got down to Dalgety Bay again. Roger Marsh was still in and was surprised to see them again.

'Have you found her?' he asked, his eyes wide.

'Can we come in and talk?' Alex asked in a quiet voice.

'Yes, yes, of course, come in.' Marsh stepped back and let them into the house, and they went back into the living room, where they had been not so long ago.

'Sit down, Mr Marsh,' Max said.

Marsh sat and looked up at them like a little boy who'd just been caught with his hand in the cookie jar. 'Is she dead?'

'Not that we know of.' The detectives stood looking at him.

'What's wrong then?'

'We're wondering why you didn't tell us about Amy Dunn.' Max stared at him, looking for a reaction and getting one.

Marsh's face turned red and he looked away. 'Amy who?' he said, facing them again.

'Listen, we've had more arrogant people than you in an interview room,' Alex said, 'and they were far better liars than you. So why don't you cut the crap and tell us why you didn't mention her.'

'Did she tell you about us?'

Max looked at Alex before answering. 'She's dead.'

Marsh jumped up so fast that Max thought he was squaring up to him. 'Dead? What do you mean, she's dead?'

'She was murdered, Mr Marsh,' Alex said. 'But we think you know about that.'

'Murdered? When?' Marsh was raising his voice now and desperately looking at them for an answer.

'She was found dead in the Cairngorms,' Max said. 'She had been murdered up there and left like a piece of rubbish.'

'Oh, Jesus,' Marsh said, sitting back down and putting his head in his hands. Then he was racked with sobs. They let him cry until he stopped. When he took his hands away, his eyes were red.

'What was she doing up in the Cairngorms?' he asked.

'I was hoping you could tell us,' Max said.

'I don't know.'

'She was killed up at one of the royal cairns.'

'Oh my God.' Marsh looked at them both for an answer but wasn't given one. 'I didn't kill her. I loved her,' he said.

'Help us understand,' Max said.

'I was in love with Amy. We met at the Kirkcaldy Galleries. I was meeting my dad for a coffee and we went in there as usual, and Amy was serving behind the counter. I started talking to her and we got on like a house on fire. Soon I was going up there on my day off just to see her. We started an affair. She wanted me to leave my wife. I told her I would, I just needed time. She said that was fine, but we shouldn't see each other until I told Helen, in case Helen went nuts. I told her I would do it this week and then I'd leave Helen and move in with Amy in Kirkcaldy. I would get a transfer over here from Edinburgh. She was excited and so was I. She was pregnant. Helen's never wanted kids, but Amy was excited.'

Max sat down on a chair and Alex followed suit.

'Have you killed Helen?' Max asked.

'What? No! Oh God, no! I was going to ask her for a divorce. I was going to sign this house over to her and she could have what she wanted. I just wanted to be with Amy.'

'You ever been in London?' Alex asked.

Marsh nodded. 'A couple of times, with Helen, a few years ago. Christmastime. And once for her birthday.'

'You said you knew about her mother being missing,' Max said. 'This seems like a hell of a coincidence, Helen going missing as well.'

'Well, that was hardly me. I was a boy when her mother went missing.'

'Maybe you got the idea from that,' Alex said.

'Look, you have to understand, I wanted to be with Amy. I was going to walk away from this life to be with her.' All the air seemed to leave Marsh. 'Now she's dead and Helen's missing. It's almost as if somebody's setting me up.'

'Let's just say somebody *was* trying to set you up; who do you think it would be?'

'I don't know.'

'Friends? Family member with a grudge? Colleague?' Alex said.

'I have a few friends, nobody who would do

something like this. Few family members. As for colleagues, well, I come into contact with a lot of people. I don't know who would want to set me up.'

'Have you had an argument with anybody recently?'

'No. I would remember.'

'We're going to ask you to give us a sample of your DNA. We have a kit in the car.'

'Anything you want. DNA, fingerprints, you can have it, if it helps you find out who killed my Amy.'

Alex went out to the car and came back with the kit and she swabbed Marsh before putting it away safely.

'We'll be in touch, Mr Marsh,' Max said, 'but you should have been honest with us from the beginning.'

Marsh stood up slowly. 'You know how that looks. Husband has girlfriend, husband's wife goes missing and more often than not ends up being found dead, husband was having an affair: husband's guilty. But I'm not guilty. I'm an A&E doctor; I've seen how badly women have been beaten. I've seen things that would make your stomach turn. I couldn't have harmed Helen. Or Amy. I loved Helen at one time, but now I love Amy. I'll always love Amy. Even when Helen comes back, I'm moving on.'

'We'll be in touch, Mr Marsh,' Max said.

He and Alex left the house and felt the cool air coming in off the sea.

'Do you think he killed her?' Max asked.

'My gut says no. I think he was genuinely wanting to move on with Amy.'

'If anybody is trying to set him up, he hasn't given us any help in identifying them.'

'I'll call Harry and update him. Maybe he could scout around at the Royal.'

'Good idea. Meantime, we'll get this sample along to Dunfermline. Let them process it.'

Alex drove away, thinking about Amy Dunn being pregnant and what she could have had if somebody hadn't snuffed out her life.

TWENTY-FOUR

'In the name of Christ,' Ewan Gallagher said, looking at his phone and shaking his head. He was the second in charge in the pathology lab of the Sick Kids' hospital at the Royal Infirmary in Edinburgh.

'What are you whining about now?' Bingo said, coming over.

Ewan looked at the smaller man wearing red glasses.

'You know something, when the fucking dead rise up again, I'm going to throw you at them so I can escape. Not that there's much meat on your bones, but it'll distract them.'

'Was that Chrissie again?' Bingo asked.

'Aye, it fucking was. You'll never guess; she told me she's pregnant and the kid is mine.'

'You're jesting.'

'Of course I'm not jesting. That's the fifth time she's sent me a text today. I thought you said she was a nice lassie?'

'She is a nice lassie,' Bingo said, his face full of mock indignation. 'She just has some problems. I thought she was over them, mind. But give her another chance. You're the one who wanted me to ask her along for a night out.'

Ewan shook his head and put his phone away. 'I tried putting the bastard thing on silent, but what if my old man falls down the stairs or something?'

'You live in a bungalow.'

'There's a room upstairs.'

'Your brother Simon lives up there.'

'But still. Joe might go snooping. You know what a nosy old bastard he is.'

'Come on, pal, give her another go. Lexi is giving me the cool treatment just now; she doesn't approve of the way you're treating her sister.'

'Me?' Ewan said, raising his voice. Some of the other workers looked over. He lowered his voice. 'I treated her like a lady. When we went to the pictures, she didn't have to put her hand in her pocket for the popcorn. That was my treat, and trust me, that bastard stuff isn't cheap. We could have had a meal in Miller and Carter for less. And when I asked her if she wanted a Pepsi, she said no, but then she bugged me about letting me give her a sip of mine. You know I don't share, especially when a lassie has a fucking shiver on her lip.'

'You didn't give her a drink?'

'What do you not understand about a lassie having a shiver on her lip? Of course you'd kiss a toilet seat.'

'That's nasty.'

'I let her keep the Pepsi, telling her I wasn't thirsty anymore.'

'So you jacked her in because she had a cold sore?' Bingo said. 'That's shallow, mate, even for you.'

'Of course that's not why I called it a day. She had annoying wee habits.'

'Like what?'

'Like calling me a dick when she's had one too many. Criticising me for the slightest thing. She's a nasty piece of work when she gets going.'

'She has her quirks.'

'Quirks?' Ewan said. 'She told the taxi driver the other night she'd boot his baws if he took the long way. And don't even get me started on her fucking kids.'

'They're wee angels.'

'Wee bastards more like. I slept over at her place one time and that was enough. She doesn't have a shower and she said I would have to have a bath. Which was fine, but she used it first and I had to use the same water, she said. Fuck that for a laugh.'

'That does sound minging right enough.'

'Listen, Bingo, Chrissie's a nutcase. I'm not going back out with her. Sorry about you and Lexi, but if I stayed with Chrissie, my life would be over.'

'Don't worry about it, mate. Lexi said she won't come near me until things get sorted with you and her sister, so I guess I'm fucked now.' Bingo shrugged his shoulders in his lab coat. 'Too bad, but I'm moving on.'

'Really?' said Ewan. 'I thought you were broken up about it?'

'I am. I hurt inside, but I'm hiding it well.'

Caroline, one of the new girls in the lab, walked up to Bingo and stopped. 'We still on for tonight?'

'Oh, ha-ha,' he said. 'The boss is looking for you.'

She giggled as she walked away.

'Ya manky bastard,' Ewan said.

'She's just having a laugh.'

'You're seeing her, aren't you?'

'We just had a drink or two,' Bingo said.

'Drowning my sorrows until Lexi comes to her senses.'

'I thought you said she'd cut it off if she found you messing about?'

'I don't think things will work out with her now, so what the eyes don't see, the heart doesn't grieve over.'

'So let me get this straight: you want me to go out with Chrissie in the hopes that Lexi will take you back, but in the meantime you're keeping it warm with the new lassie.'

'Pretty much.'

'Dirty wee bastard.'

'Aye, who am I kidding; Chrissie is one Class-A psycho. But in my own defence, I didn't know that when I was going out with Lexi. I'd only met the lassie once, and her heid was hanging out a taxi as she let one go.'

Ewan screwed his face up. 'God Almighty. You could have warned me.'

'You're the one who insisted on me asking her out for you. "Let's do a foursome," you said. Look how that worked out; she got pished in the golf club and asked the bar steward for a fight.'

'I thought she was just a wee bit drunk.'

'You're lucky you didn't get us barred.'

'What about this crap about her being pregnant?'

'She's just trying to get money out of you, if you want my opinion. Or to get you running back to her. Just ignore her and she'll move on to the next sucker.'

'It's put me off dating, let me tell you,' Ewan said, fishing his phone out of his pocket again.

'Has it?'

'Of course not. But let me ask you: do you think Lexi was put off by you wearing your red sunglasses all the time? Because if not, I was thinking of getting a pair.'

'They're glasses, ya bastard. And you'd look like a film star with them on.'

'You think so?'

'Aye. Rebel Wilson.'

'She lost a lot of weight, smartarse.' Ewan looked at his phone again. 'Christ Almighty.'

'What is it now?'

'DCI Harry McNeil is asking if I'm working today. He wants a word.'

'Tell him to fuck off. That's what I would do. And to his face.'

'Let's see you then.'

'What do you mean?'

'He's standing over there inside the door.'

TWENTY-FIVE

1985

He was sitting watching cartoons when the door opened. Watching cartoons and eating a bowl of cereal for dinner again.

He heard the sound of cursing as his old man came staggering up the hallway, banging off the walls. He felt the hairs on the back of his neck stand on end again. Just like the last time, and the time before that.

The last time his father had come home drunk, he had forced himself on the boy. He had screamed as his father had pulled his trousers down, but a big, hairy hand had covered his mouth until it was over.

He'd had to stay off school for three days after that last time.

Now he was coming again, and the boy started shaking. The cereal he was eating was spilling out of the bowl onto the settee. He couldn't control his legs, and then he started crying, despite telling himself he wouldn't do that again.

'Where the fuck are you?' his father said. His suit was crumpled and stained on the front as if he'd puked over himself again. His belly was straining at the waist. His tie was undone and his hair was dishevelled.

'Get through to that room,' the big man said, leaning against the doorjamb.

'I'm watching cartoons,' the boy said, trying to keep the shaking from his voice, but it was hard. He wished more than anything that his mum was here so she could stop his father. He missed her more than anything.

'What did you fucking say?' The monster stood upright and was about to take a step into the living room when he felt something slap him hard against the back of his legs.

'What the fuck?' he shouted, turning round to see what had hit him. Or who.

The boy – who was *the man* now, a big strapping man – was standing looking at him.

'Hello there.' He smiled and put the cricket bat over his shoulder.

'I'm going to kill you,' the drunk said.

The hallway was tight, but you didn't need to swing the bat like a roundhouse punch to do damage. As the drunk walked towards the man, the man brought the bat down hard and fast on top of the drunk's head, just above his brow. This brought the drunk to his knees, but before he could keel over, the man stepped forward and threw the bat onto the floor of the bedroom on his right and grabbed the drunk, pulling him to his feet again. There was no blood, just a daze brought on by the strike and the alcohol abuse.

'Get the door,' the man said to the little boy, who was now standing, watching.

'Is...is it going to be okay?'

'Yes. Just stick to the story we talked about and I promise you it will be okay.'

The man had connections. He would make sure the boy was put in a loving foster home. And he'd be checking all the time to make sure the foster parents were looking after the boy.

The man put one of the drunk's arms around his

shoulders and helped him outside, like they were two buds going for a drink. He helped him over to his car and put him on the back seat. If he got pulled over, he would say the drunk was a friend and he was driving the friend home.

But he didn't get pulled over that night. And the drunk went away for good. And the little boy got to live with a nice family, and the man did indeed check on him all the time. He was like a big brother.

And he never forgot him.

TWENTY-SIX

'I know this is becoming a habit,' Harry said to Ewan Gallagher as they sat down at a table in the canteen.

'My reputation is shot round here, so having a cop come and question me on a regular basis won't make much difference.'

'Love life not doing so good?' Harry asked.

'Usual story: waiting for the right one to come along.'

'Hang in there. She'll come along.'

'That was a shock with Morgan Allan. I read about it in the news.'

'It was a shock for me too.' Harry debated whether to talk about Alex or not, but thought it might be best if he got straight to the point. 'I want to ask you if you know a doctor, Roger Marsh?'

'Marshie-boy? Of course I do. Everybody knows him. He works in A&E.'

'What's he like?'

'Christ, how long have you got? He's conceited, arrogant, loaded and likes to think he's God's gift.'

'Not a pleasant man, then?'

Ewan sipped his coffee. 'To be honest, I think he likes to give off this aura that he's a big, bad guy, but I think he's all mouth and no trousers. He had an argument with Bingo one night in the pub. We were on a work night out and we just happened to bump into him and some of the other toffs from here, and he was giving it laldy with the mouth, slagging off Bingo. You know what it's like with some guys and the drink: one minute they're having a laugh, the next they're wanting to go boxing. But Marshie didn't get like that, more like he was just in the mood for winding somebody up without wanting to take his head off. Bingo, on the other hand, wanted to take him outside. I stopped him.

'But it would have served Marshie right if he'd got his teeth knocked out. In A&E he talks to people like they're scum. Nobody likes him. He has no respect for anybody, so nobody has any respect for him. One day, a few months ago, I was down there, and he ripped into an ambulance driver. Martin, his name is. Good guy. We've met him a few times. I couldn't believe the way Marshie spoke to him. Then there was a nurse who got a tongue-lashing from him. I mean, I'm not saying he isn't good at his job, but he has no personality. Rumour has it he was looking to transfer to Fife. And good riddance to him.'

'What about his wife, Helen?'

'I saw in the papers that she's missing,' Ewan said. 'If you ask me, she probably did a runner just to get away from him. I don't blame her.'

'There's no evidence of that.'

'She probably found out he was seeing that other woman. Everybody knew about it. And Marshie's wife worked here, so she might have heard the rumours too. Some lassie from Fife. She worked here part time in the café. Amy. She was a nice lassie, and God knows what she saw in Marshie, but rumour had it, they were seeing each other. Marshie was in here a lot after Amy started working here.'

'He seemed to treat her well?' Harry asked, not touching his coffee.

'I would say so. They seemed to like each other's company.'

'Good to hear. We're just looking into something, that's why I was asking your opinion.'

'Nae bother. But here, how's Sticks? You know

her, don't you? She works in the mortuary. I saw
Martin bringing her into A&E. She's a good laugh.'

'I'm not sure,' Harry said. 'She collapsed at a
crime scene. She's a bit under the weather.'

'She's an awfy lassie. Talk about people cheating
on their spouses; I can't get a girlfriend just now,
never mind get one if I was married.'

'Sticks is going with a married man?'

'Aye. She swore me and Bingo to secrecy.'

'And here you are telling me,' Harry said.

'You're the one asking all the questions about my
co-workers and friends.'

'Touché.'

'But yeah,' Ewan said, 'Sticks let it slip that she's
seeing somebody and he's going to be leaving his
wife, but aren't they all? They just give women a line
to get what they want. But I hope she's okay. She's a
nice lassie.'

'I've known her for years. And Gus Weaver too,
of course.'

'Aye, Gus. Good lad. He never married. He told
us that in the pub one night. He couldn't find the
right woman, he said. Likes to play the field, I think.'

They chatted for a little while longer, then Harry
stood up. 'Once again, I'm indebted to you for your
help.'

'Aye, the Royal is a hotbed of action, let me tell you. When you work behind the scenes like me, you get to see a lot of stuff. I'm always walking about to wards and talking to doctors, so I get to hear a lot of stuff whether I want to or not.'

'Thanks again, Ewan.' Harry shook the younger man's hand and started walking away, but then he stopped. 'Your pal's still going with the red sunglasses, I see.'

'Christ, don't call them sunglasses. They're "glasses" according to him. What a laddie.'

Harry chuckled as he left the café.

TWENTY-SEVEN

Harry walked along to the Accident and Emergency department. It was busy with some ambulances sitting outside.

He saw Martin Cross, the ambulance driver, standing next to his ambulance.

'Hi, Martin.'

Cross turned round to look at Harry. 'Oh, hi there, Harry.'

'I thought I would check in and see how Sticks is doing.'

'They took her in a wee while ago. I think she just fainted, but I'm only here to transport the patients. We tell the doctors what we did, but it's frowned upon to give a medical opinion.'

Harry nodded. 'I was talking to somebody about

Roger Marsh, one of the doctors here. Do you know him?'

Cross nodded. 'I do. He knows his stuff, no doubt about that, but he has no personality. He likes to order people about and talks to them like they're shit.'

'I don't suppose he has many friends here.'

'He has a few girlfriends, that's for sure. From what I've heard. We stand around here and people get talking when they're bored. Marsh is a player. He was cheating on his wife, so I heard. With some girl who worked here. Abby something, Amy, something like that. I spoke to her a couple of times. I don't know what she sees in Marsh. Probably his earnings. You know what some women are like.'

'I read the report on Paul Hart being brought here,' Harry said. 'He was with some prison officers.'

'Aye, I saw them hovering about on the ward. I had to wheel an old boy upstairs. One of them got a bit shirty with me. What was the idiot's name again? Todd. He started throwing his weight about, got really nasty. I told him I work here all the time, bringing in patients, while he was just here for a wee holiday. He didn't like that.' Cross chuckled. 'He's a real hard man. I overheard a couple of the guys talking; seems like Todd was having it away with some-body. I don't know what it is nowadays.'

'A place like this is rife with people having affairs, I think.'

Cross looked at his watch. 'I'm knocking off now. Good talking with you again, Chief Inspector.'

Harry walked into the hospital and went up to reception and showed the woman his warrant card.

'I'm enquiring about a woman who was brought in here. Her name is Natalie. I'm not sure of her second name, but she's Polish and works in the city mortuary.'

'Let me have a look for you,' the woman replied. Then after a couple of minutes on the keyboard, she looked at Harry. 'She was discharged a little while ago. Nothing serious. A fainting spell.'

'Thank you,' Harry said and he left, feeling relieved that Sticks was okay.

As he drove down to Fettes, he thought about calling Alex, but he realised she might feel he was being too protective, so he left it.

The team were in the incident room, Skellett sitting with one of his legs up on a chair.

Lillian O'Shea was at the whiteboard, sticking photos on it.

'Harry, son, how did you get on with that laddie, Ewan?' Stewart asked.

'He told me that Marsh does not get on well with others. I also spoke to the ambulance driver, Martin Cross, who took Sticks to the hospital, and he confirmed that Marsh is a real ball-buster. Alex said Marsh was a basket case when they interviewed him, but that isn't what he's like every day.'

'So this Amy Dunn was attracted to him?' Skellett said.

'Apparently,' Harry answered. 'Maybe he's charming when he's outside work.'

'What do we have on his wife, apart from the fact that she's missing?' Stewart asked.

'Nothing. She's a nurse at the Royal, along with Marsh. A nice woman by all accounts.'

Stewart looked at Elvis. 'What do we have on the friends of Marion Todd, our Roseburn victim?'

'We located the friend who lives on Roseburn Street. She said that Marion was the first one to leave. She was going to walk down to the tram stop at Murrayfield Stadium.'

'Did you get the names of the others?'

'I did. We ran a background check, and they're all clean. No records for anything.'

Frank Miller walked across to the board. 'All

their alibis checked out. We contacted the taxi office who sent the taxis and they all went home to their addresses.'

'How long after Marion left did they leave?'

'About an hour, according to the taxi record.'

'Why did Marion leave earlier than the others?' Harry asked Miller.

'The friend said Marion went into the bathroom to make a call and it was a bit heated. Then she seemed a bit angry when she came out. She didn't say anything.'

'We looked at Michael Todd's phone today,' Stewart said, 'and it shows he called his wife at around ten thirty. He started his shift at eleven.'

'Was her phone found at the scene?' Harry asked.

'No. No phone, handbag, nothing,' Elvis said.

'Do we have a warrant to track her phone?' Stewart asked.

'Already in the works,' Elvis said.

'Michael Todd gave a statement and submitted his DNA and his alibi checks out,' Lillian said.

'Did any of the women leave the party at all after Marion left?' Miller asked.

'No, they all gave each other an alibi,' Lillian said.

'Marion's husband was one of the guards with Paul Hart and now she's been murdered by his protégé?' Harry said. 'I think she was targeted, maybe to get revenge on Todd.'

'Somebody would have to know that Todd was one of the guards who escorted Hart to the hospital,' Harry said. 'Somebody who was close to them in the hospital.'

'We can check out the other guards tomorrow,' Miller said.

TWENTY-EIGHT

Sticks hated herself for fainting at the crime scene. She had been to so many that it was second nature to her. She had never felt sick or passed out before, but seeing the woman's face looking up at her had made her insides tumble. Marion Todd.

She shook her head as she parked her car in the mortuary car park. She had called Kate Murphy and told her she would be in for the on-call shift. Gus wouldn't have to worry about covering for her. She had let the team down today, but she wouldn't let them down tonight.

She would get inside, get the kettle on and call her boyfriend again. She'd called him just before she had left for work and they'd argued. She had been expecting him to call, and he had told her, 'My wife just died; don't be such a selfish bitch.' Then he had dumped her. She had cried and cried and had tried to call him back, but to no avail. She would call him again.

Inside, it was quiet, except for the gentle hum of the refrigerators. She went upstairs to the locker room and hung up her jacket, and then she took a small Bluetooth speaker from her bag and carried it back down to the break room, where she put the kettle on.

Her stomach was in knots. She couldn't get Marion Todd's face out of her mind. The poor woman. Her face would haunt Sticks for the rest of her life.

Then the doubts hit her again, just like they had this morning. The questions that had run through her mind, making her sick until she passed out.

What if? She started thinking like that now. She had to shake it off, but it was the quiet in here that was sending her thoughts in all the directions they shouldn't be going.

She made a call. It went to voicemail. 'I'm on call tonight. I'm at the mortuary right now. Please come see me. I need to talk to you.'

She hung up and felt sick, wondering if she had done the right thing. It was too late now; she'd made the call, so now she would wait and see if he turned up.

She set her speaker up, put on a podcast and waited for the kettle to boil.

She listened to true crime podcasts; that was her problem. Crime was never too far away, both in her private life and in her working life. She was thinking maybe she should change her career path. Maybe go back to working in the hospital where she had started before taking this job. Working a normal nine-to-five job, with the occasional on-call shift. Working with a lot more people. She liked the people in here, but maybe it was working with death all the time that dragged her down.

Then she heard a noise.

A clink, like somebody had dropped a scalpel.

He had come after all. Just like she'd known he would. She would talk to him, tell him her fears, and hope to God he wasn't responsible, but he would have to convince her.

Or else she would talk to Harry McNeil. Or Frank Miller.

She couldn't go on like this. She had to know.

She got up from the break room and walked to the refrigeration room, where he was waiting.

TWENTY-NINE

Alex had insisted on cooking, sweet and sour chicken on rice.

'I cooked a lot,' she told Harry. Grace was in her highchair, waving a spoon about.

The kitchen smelled good as Harry tried to fight off the weird feeling he had. For the longest time, he had wondered what it would be like if there had been a mistake and Alex was really still alive, recovering from some kind of injury as she slowly regained her memory. How he would react when she came home. Imagination was very different from reality. He had a million questions he wanted to ask her.

Jessica had gone out for a drink with some of her friends from the nursery, leaving them alone.

Harry didn't want to keep bringing things up, but he couldn't help himself.

'Did you think about us a lot, or did we fade over time?' he asked her, drinking from a bottle of beer.

Alex turned to face him. 'I thought about you all day every day. That's why I came down to Edinburgh. I wanted to see you and Grace so much. I thought, to hell with it, I'm going back to Harry, but I didn't want to put Grace in danger.' She looked at him. 'Did you think of me?'

He couldn't answer for a moment, trying to formulate an answer that would adequately describe his feelings for her at the time.

'I can't begin to describe how much I missed you. I even thought about ending things, if I'm honest. I ran away, bought the place down south and didn't know what to do with myself. Then a young officer and her family came into my life, DI Lisa McDonald. They gave me purpose again. I knew I had to come home for Grace. So yes, I thought about you nonstop, dreaming of this day, knowing it would never happen.'

She walked over and held him, then parted, kissing him. 'I'm back for good, Harry.'

'That's good to hear.'

They ate dinner and watched some TV, and then

Alex bathed Grace. Harry was thinking about Marion Todd, thinking about Paul Hart and how the man had ended up in hospital not once, not twice, but three times with a heart attack.

Then Harry's phone rang.

'Harry? It's Kate Murphy. We have a problem.'

THIRTY

It wasn't like the movies, where the damsel in distress waits on the hero to arrive and meantime the killer takes her out too.

After Harry spoke to Kate Murphy, he called control and had a patrol car pick her up and take her to the mortuary, and he left instructions that they should wait for him.

And so they were waiting for him outside in the car park when he arrived.

'No answer still?' he asked Kate after getting out of his car.

She had got out of the patrol car along with the officers when his car came in and parked.

'Nothing. I've been trying to get a hold of her. I asked her if she would be okay tonight and she said she would be fine. Gus could have taken over for her. He's not answering his phone either. I would have come here myself, but after what happened to Andy, the way he was murdered, I've been scared to go out on my own. Even though there's no threat to me...' She trailed off and looked at Harry sheepishly.

'You don't have to explain. It happens to a lot of the spouses of victims. It makes you feel unsettled. But we're here now.'

'Thank you,' Kate said in a low voice.

'Let's see if the door's locked,' Harry said, indicating for one of the uniforms to try the handle. It was unlocked.

'Right, let's get inside.'

The uniforms led the way.

'Kate, stay behind. If shit gets real, run like...well, you know, run,' Harry said.

'I will.'

Harry took his baton out of its holster under his jacket. Lights were on in the refrigeration room, as expected. It was empty. They walked through to the break room. Nobody was there. There was no sign that anybody had been here recently.

The uniforms searched the building, but it was empty.

'Call her number, Kate,' Harry said.

Kate took her phone out and dialled the number. It rang and went to voicemail. She hung up and looked at Harry, her face going pale.

'You need to hear this, Harry.' She dialled the number again and put the phone on speaker, and they both listened to the voicemail greeting.

'I need to speak to you. Call me.'

'Right. I'll make some phone calls. We'll go and pick this bastard up.'

THIRTY-ONE

Michael Todd was just getting ready to leave for work when there was a knock on his front door.

'Christ, who the hell is this?' he said, walking from the living room to open the door.

Being a prison officer, his reflexes were fast, but not on a par with the armed officers who barged their way in, pointing their Heckler and Koch machine guns in his face.

He tripped over his own feet and landed on his back and looked down the barrel of a gun.

'Well, well, Michael Todd, we meet again,' Calvin Stewart said. 'Guess what we've got?'

Todd lay on his back as uniforms piled in, along with plain clothes officers.

'No? A fucking search warrant, and just to

double up the prize, an arrest warrant. Roll over, you're under arrest.'

'For what?' Todd screamed.

'Get him up on his feet,' Stewart said, and uniforms squeezed by while the firearms team covered him.

They cuffed him and got him to his feet.

'Michael Todd, I'm arresting you for the murder of your wife,' Stewart said as Harry went into the living room. Stewart finished reading Todd his rights and the man was roughly taken from his house.

'He's shouting like a wee lassie,' Charlie Skellett said, coming into the house. 'Did I miss anything?'

'Like what?' Stewart said.

'Like you booting him in the baws.'

'You're being ridiculous now. Confusing me with yourself, Charlie.'

Skellett chuckled. 'Dearie me, so I am.' He winked at Stewart.

Stewart tutted and walked into the living room. 'We're going to tear this whole place apart,' he said to Harry. 'I'm leaving Charlie in charge. You and me will go and talk to Todd at the station.'

'Everything looks so normal. You would hardly think a serial killer lives here.'

'You can never tell, Harry, son.'

Todd's clothes had been taken from him and he was wearing tracksuit bottoms and a sweatshirt. A solicitor sat next to him, an older man who couldn't have looked more bored if he tried.

Harry and Stewart sat opposite Todd, the recorder sitting on the table to one side. The camera up in the corner was all-seeing.

They started the recording process before Stewart spoke.

'Where's Natalie?' he said.

'Who?'

'You know her as Sticks. The mortuary assistant,' Harry said. 'Your girlfriend.'

'I don't have a girlfriend.'

'We know Natalie is your girlfriend. She recorded a new voicemail greeting. It was quite explicit; in it she tells you to call her or she's going to the police. She knows what you've done. Sounds to me like she knows you killed your wife. Is that why you went along to talk to her tonight? To talk to her?'

'I haven't spoken to her.'

'This is what we're thinking,' Harry said, 'but feel free to correct us if we've got it wrong. She somehow found out that you killed Marion. You had drawn a love heart on her chest to make it look like the work of somebody who had been working with Paul Hart. You know the man, don't you? The man you had conversations with in the hospital when you were guarding him. Did he give you some tips?'

'I didn't talk to him. I don't know what you're talking about.'

'Maybe you overheard him talking. Paul Hart loved the sound of his own voice. That's what his cellmate, Hughes, said.'

Todd looked at Harry without saying a word, so the detective carried on. 'His signature. Michael, that's why you drew a heart on your wife's chest after you killed her. You knew that was what Hart drew on his victims.'

'Come on,' the solicitor said. 'Do you have any proof?'

'Not exactly proof,' Stewart said, 'more of a mistake on Michael's part.'

'What do you mean?' Todd said now, intrigued.

'You see, when you drew the heart on her chest, it was filled in. A nice little red love heart drawn on her chest with lipstick. We're testing all her lipsticks for fingerprints. They've been bagged and they'll be taken away to the lab. Will we find your prints on one, Michael?'

'So what? I dust the bedroom. My fingerprints will be on one. Of course it will.'

'Just one? If you dust, your prints will be on more than just one, surely?' Harry said. 'But we're getting ahead of ourselves here, Michael. You see, your love heart was different from Paul Hart's; he only drew an outline. He never coloured the heart in with lipstick. In fact, he never used lipstick at all. He always used a red marker pen. Harder to come off, he said.'

'Fuck,' Todd said.

'Don't say anything else,' his solicitor advised.

'Shut up,' Todd snarled at the man. 'That stupid bastard should have made things clearer.'

'Did you kill your wife, Michael?' Stewart said.

Todd nodded. 'Marion wasn't going to give me a divorce. She knew about us. In fact, she'd had it out with Sticks. Natalie, I mean. She got in her face one day. Told Natalie she would never divorce me.'

'Then you decided to get rid of Marion?'

'Yes.'

'Hart wouldn't have told anybody his secret,' Harry said. 'So how did you find out?'

'I was listening at the door one day when he was talking. I thought I could use it to my advantage. But as I said, Hart wasn't specific. I thought he'd said he used lipstick.'

'Have you done anything to Natalie?' Stewart said, trying to throw Todd off balance.

'What? No, of course not. I wanted to spend the rest of my life with her.'

'She changed her voicemail greeting to record a message for you; she wanted you to call her. She knows what you've done.'

'Impossible. Natalie and I use disposable phones. If she wanted to call me, she could have just called me on the disposable. Especially now that Marion isn't here. She wouldn't have used my regular phone.'

'You said you were listening to Hart in the hospital,' Harry said. 'Was he just talking to himself?'

Todd shook his head. 'No. He was talking to his accomplice. The man I thought I could blame for Marion's murder. The man you're looking for.'

'Who is it?'

He told them and they ended the interview.

THIRTY-TWO

It was a small house outside Livingston, in a quiet little street. It was semi-detached and seemed decent enough. Tonight was going to change all of that. The house was going to be headline news tomorrow.

The takedown had been put together at lightning speed, but considering who they were going to take down, it was put together very well.

DSup Lynn McKenzie stood next to Stewart, out of sight of their target.

Stewart introduced her to Superintendent Bob Dolan, who was in charge of this operation. The firearms teams were in place, uniforms were round the back, the dog handlers were round the corner waiting on the shout.

'You're Glasgow Division, Calvin told me,' Dolan said.

'Yes. I'm liaising with DSup Stewart as we found things in one of Hart's old houses. Ground-penetrating radar showed nothing at that address.'

'We might get lucky with this one then,' Dolan said, then spoke into his radio. 'Positive sighting on the ground floor. Living room.'

'Then let's hit it,' Stewart said, and Dolan gave the word to go.

Both front and back doors were taken off their hinges at the same time before the armed teams rushed in. The vans came round with the dogs and a whole bunch of uniforms stormed the house.

For the second time that night, Harry and Stewart entered a home in a flash.

'Martin Cross, I'm arresting you for the murder of Amy Dunn,' Stewart said, and went through his whole spiel again.

Cross looked different without his paramedic's uniform on.

'What's going on?' he said, surprise on his face.

'Cut the shite, son,' Stewart said. 'Don't you remember when you put the newspaper clippings into those photo frames in the house in Wishaw for us to find? Don't you think we'll find fingerprints on them? Never mind if we don't. But you should have paid more attention to the names in the frames that Hart asked you to leave up in the attic in Wishaw. He lived here. One of those three lassies was from Livingston, not Wishaw. Paul Hart was a builder, and this place was searched but nothing found. However, he was clever, and when we got the planning officer out of his bed a wee while ago, we found permits for the extension at the back. With a poured concrete floor. We're going to rip it up.'

'That means fuck all!' Cross shouted. 'I'm only renting this place.'

'Renting it from who? It's owned by Paul Hart, so you must be renting it from him. But the way we see it, son, is Paul Hart wasn't going to his grave without taking you down with him. He played games. He was selfish, so every decision he made was for himself, nobody else.' Stewart smiled at Cross.

'He's the one who wanted Amy Dunn dead after I told him I saw her in the Royal Infirmary. He planned it all. I just carried it out.'

'We can hardly arrest him now that he's dead,' Stewart said.

Cross smiled like a madman. 'I suppose I'll get all the credit now, right enough.'

'We also got your accomplice, Michael Todd,' Harry said.

'Who?' Cross said, and a chill went up Harry's neck. 'I don't know anybody called Michael Todd. If he told you he worked with me, he's a liar! He's just trying to grab the glory! We won't let him do that!'

'*We?* Who's we, Martin? Not Paul Hart, obviously, but somebody else.'

Cross said nothing.

'You're willing to go down for your partner? So he can carry on killing, like you were supposed to be doing?' Stewart said. 'He'll have all the fun while you rot in prison for the rest of your life. I've no doubt that we'll get him one day, but meantime you'll be sitting inside reading about him, knowing all the time it could have been you. Tell us who he is and we'll make sure he never has any fun again.'

Cross thought about it and nodded.

And told them who they were looking for.

THIRTY-THREE

It was late, and Harry was at the stage where he was buzzed and needed to sleep. It had been a long night and he was feeling knackered, but this had to be done.

He sat in the darkness, the heat from the log fire seeping into him. He had looked at his watch a few minutes ago and thought the person he was expecting wasn't going to show, that maybe he'd got it wrong.

Then he heard the front door being slowly opened. This was an old house and sound carried easily in the dark silence of the night.

He heard soft footsteps on the stone hallway floor before the living room door opened. The lights weren't on, but he could easily make out the features of the man from the light of the blazing log fire. Harry had made sure to keep feeding it.

'Come in. Have a seat by the fire,' he said to the man.

Gus Weaver stood looking at him. 'What are you doing here?'

'I thought we could sit down and have a nice wee cup of tea.'

Weaver walked to the opposite end of the fireplace and picked up a poker. 'It was silly of you to come.'

'Really? I just wanted to ask if there was anything you wanted to get off your chest before I take you back over to Edinburgh. This is a nice place you have here, Gus. Little cottage in the middle of nowhere in Fife. Perfect for your needs, isn't it?'

'I don't know what you're talking about.' Weaver stepped forward and poked at the logs, making sparks fly.

'Really? You didn't abduct Sticks tonight and bring her here? They're both safe, you know, Sticks and Helen Marsh. I'm surprised that you let Helen live.'

Gus smiled. 'She was three when we killed her mother. Paul and me. I mean, I just helped him, but I felt like I was a killer then. It started when he told me

I could get away with killing my abusive sister. And I did. They thought it was an accident. That felt so good. If you've never killed somebody, you should try it.'

Harry thought back to what Hart's cellmate had said: Hart had said he had killed his sister, despite not having one. He had actually been talking as if he was Gus Weaver killing his sister, reliving the memory of a young Gus making his first kill.

'My sister was abusive, to both me and my mother. Nobody missed her, except for maybe her dad. I wish I'd killed him too.'

'What about Martin Cross? How did he come into the picture?'

'He was a neighbour. I was a man when I first got involved with him. His mother had died and his father was an abusive drunk. He raped Martin when he was drunk, and it was happening more and more, so I killed him and took him away and buried him in the woods. And after that, I looked out for Martin. Educated him.'

'And you've both been killing for a very long time,' Harry said, slowly getting to his feet.

'We have. You'll have to go back to all the missing women you have on file and see which ones we killed. Martin is good at it. He'll show up at a scene and figure out who he's going to go back for. It's a skill with him. But I'm guessing you have him in custody already. Too bad.'

Harry tried to read Weaver's face illuminated by the flickering glow from the fire. He could only see madness there.

'Why didn't you kill Helen Hunt when you had the chance? Or do you keep them for a while before killing them?' Harry asked.

'She got in my head. She kept talking about when she was a little girl. She remembered going onto the walkway with me and Paul. Remembered watching us throwing her mother over the allotment wall. Three years old and she could remember! I tried to kill her, but I just couldn't bring myself to do it.'

'What about Amy Dunn?' Harry asked Weaver.

'Martin recognised her when she was in the Royal. She worked in the café there and she was a chatty woman. Martin was there and she was talking to him, and that's when he recognised her from the days when she was a witness against Paul. She was changed a little bit, the hair especially, but he knew she wasn't Amy Dunn, that she must have been put into witness protection. So he started going to the café regularly and talking to her, and then he saw her and Roger Marsh together. He asked her about Marsh and she confided in Martin that Marsh was the father of her baby. It was easy to find out where Marsh lived after that. And from there, we figured out where she lived. Then one day, she said they were going hiking in the Cairngorms. We went there too, and I slipped a little something into Marsh's drink. Martin bumped into Amy, pretending he was there with some friends. He offered to hike up to the cairn with her, and he killed her up there.'

'Michael Todd overheard you talking in Hart's room when he was standing guard outside,' Harry said. 'He killed his wife and left Hart's signature, but he got it wrong. And now the three of you are going away for murder.'

'There's no car outside, so I'm thinking you were dropped off and they're waiting at a staging area to come up here and take me away,' Weaver said. 'You know I'm not going to let that happen, Harry. You think I care if Helen and Sticks are away? There will be others. I'll make sure of that.'

Weaver made his move then, raising the poker, but before he could strike, Calvin Stewart stepped out of the shadows and threw his hot cup of tea over him. As Weaver screamed, Skellett stepped out and smacked him on the arm with his walking stick, fracturing Weaver's arm.

Harry grabbed hold of Weaver, throwing the man to the floor on his back.

'Fucking Jessie. The tea was almost cold by the time you'd stopped your fucking gums flapping.'

'Bastards. I'll kill the fucking lot of you.' Weaver struggled and kicked, even with his fractured arm.

Stewart found the light switch and the room was bathed in light.

'Nice place here, Weaver,' he said. 'But it won't be after we dig the fucking place up.'

Harry stepped back with Stewart and Skellett.

Stewart had sent a text to the patrol unit who were sitting down the road out of sight, and now flashing blue lights cut through the window just before two uniforms came in.

Weaver screamed as he was lifted to his feet.

'Better get an ambulance up here,' Harry said.

Weaver stopped struggling as he was led out.

'I don't know about you boys, but I thought that tea Weaver has was pish.'

'It is,' Stewart agreed. 'I had two cups before he turned up. I'm glad I threw the third one over the bastard.'

THIRTY-FOUR

'Gus Weaver,' Alex said again. 'He seemed like such a nice guy. Very friendly, and you could always have a laugh with him.'

'It takes all sorts,' Harry said, yawning again. It was really late now and he had left exhaustion behind a long time ago.

'You sure you don't want a coffee? I don't mind making it.'

'I'm sure. I really want to sleep. We won't be going in early.'

They were sitting at the kitchen table. Harry felt stiff and tired. He had been glad Stewart and Skellett were there as back-up.

'How's Calvin Stewart to work with?'

Harry nodded. 'He's loud, but no matter what anybody says, he gets the job done.'

'I can't wait to meet him. One day.'

'You will, Alex.' He sat back in the chair. 'This has been a hell of a few days. Once we get all the paperwork wrapped up on this one, I'm having a rest.'

'Neil said you should. You've been through a lot.'

'How did Max Hold work out?' he asked.

Alex smiled. 'He was good to work with. He was in the Met for fifteen years, but he wanted to come back home.'

'Does he have anybody here?'

'No. He's divorced. He wants to start over again.'

'Good for him.' Harry stood up. 'I need to get some sleep.'

Alex stood up. 'Me too. Grace and Jess are fast asleep, so maybe I can catch some shuteye too. I couldn't sleep knowing you were out late.'

They left the kitchen and Harry made sure the front door was locked. He'd been paranoid about that lately.

They walked up the stairs to the landing, where the bedrooms were.

Alex stopped to look at him. 'Goodnight, Harry.'

'Goodnight, Alex.'

They stood that way for a few seconds.

'You still think that maybe one day you'll be able to sleep in the same bed as me?' she asked.

He held out his hand. He'd been apart from Alex for a very long time. Now he didn't want to spend another night without her.

'Come on. Let's sit and talk for a little while. In my room,' he said. 'In our room.'

THIRTY-FIVE

He stood in the darkness, watching. The two women were brought in by ambulance. He'd almost walked into the trap when they were racing up towards Weaver's place. But he never took anything for granted and had made sure he parked well enough away and had started walking when he saw the blue flashing lights.

It had saved him.

He knew Weaver wouldn't say anything; he knew to keep quiet. Cross didn't know about him, so he was safe in that respect.

It was starting to drizzle now.

He turned away from the hospital entrance and walked back to his car.

He would lie low for a while.

Then, one day in the future, he'd be back. And he'd make sure Harry McNeil knew about it.

But for now, he merely got back in his car and drove out of the car park, and not one person who might look into his car would know that they were locking eyes with a serial killer.

The serial killer who had murdered Paul Hart in hospital.

AFTERWORD

I would like to say that when I use the term, "taking a Benny" in my books, it's slang for taking a tantrum, or going off one's head. Not taking drugs.

I would like to thank a gentleman who took some time to sit down with me and talk about my books and give me some insights. He doesn't want to be named, but he knows who he is.

niece, Lynn McKenzie Thanks to thank my. And also a huge thank you once again to Jacqueline Beard who is absolutely fantastic! And to Charlie Wilson, who deserves a medal.

Thanks to Alex who works in the Scran and Scallie restaurant in Stockbridge, Edinburgh, for taking care of us. If you haven't been there, you should try the place. It's one of the best restaurants I've been in.

And a huge thank you to all of my readers who make this all worthwhile. If you could see your way to leaving a review or a rating on Amazon, I would truly appreciate it.

Stay safe my friends.

John Carson
New York
January 2023

ABOUT THE AUTHOR

John Carson is originally from Edinburgh but now lives with his wife and family in New York State. He shares his house with four cats and two dogs.

website - johncarsonauthor.com
    Facebook - JohnCarsonAuthor
    Twitter - JohnCarsonBooks
    Instagram - JohnCarsonAuthor

Printed in Great Britain
by Amazon

29516935R00144